# The Art of Ruin

# The Art of Ruin
A novel by Rhoda Stamell

Mayapple Press 2009

© Copyright 2009 by Rhoda Stamell

Published by   MAYAPPLE PRESS
               408 N. Lincoln St.
               Bay City, MI 48708
               *www.mayapplepress.com*

ISBN 978-0932412-78-2

Second Printing

ACKNOWLEDGMENTS

The Wurlitzer Foundation in Taos, New Mexico, and The Writers Colony at Dairy Hollow in Eureka Springs, Arkansas.

Specials thanks to the Ragdale Foundation for awarding me my first residency in 1996, which was granted to women who had begun their serious writing career after the age of fifty.

Cover photo by Rhoda Stamell. Cover design by Judith Kerman. Book designed and typeset by Amee Schmidt with cover titles in Enviro, poem titles in Adobe Garamond Pro, and text in ITC Giovanni.

*This book is dedicated to my students,
1957-1997, Detroit Public Schools.*

# Chapter One: The Boyfriend Party

His name is Suliman, he says.
She says, "Solomon?"
"No, I said my name is Suliman, not Solomon. My whole life folks been telling me my name."
Kate has spent her whole life apologizing for the wrong-saying of names. The first week of each semester, reading down the list of students: Polish names, Finnish names, Italian names. Szemanski, Kopenen, Malatessio. The boys blush when she stumbles over their names, but the girls count it against her because she is sexy. It is always like that even when the names are Johnson and Williams and Cooper.
She is sexy all the time. It is her business. She teaches womanliness. Home Economics. There isn't a better name for the subject.
People call her a redhead. She is scrupulous about keeping that a fact of life with late night applications of L'Oreal.
That's her signature: red hair spilling across the crumpled pillow.
Her ankles are slim, not like the thick ankles of some teachers, standing all day, everything descending, their weight pouring into their feet. She wears an ankle bracelet. She has bought it for herself, but she wears it as if it were a trophy.
When she extends her leg, she imagines the lover running his hand over the long stretch of her leg. He turns the ankle in his hand like a sculptor admiring the work he has produced from some stubborn stone. The dream memory drifts over the classroom. The girls hate her for it.
She got left out in the body department, but she makes the best of what she has been given: the thick waist and small breasts. No butt, and black men love a "big woman."
But the careful tuning of a lifetime is not enough for this Suliman.

"Who are you with, Suliman?" She is careful not to say Solomon; her taunting days are over. Now she is at the mercy of a man when it comes to choosing. Tables have turned.

Suliman nods at a woman, blonde, tight-faced, but her neck is wrinkled like the high collar of a soft blouse, probably a face-lift. She can't see the woman clearly, but she is speculating about what Suliman, a young man, is doing with this woman. He could have been one of her students, fifteen years ago in her Life Styles class. Sex education or Sex Prohibition, where telling the truth would have gotten her suspended or at least reprimanded.

He is definitely from the street, with wardrobe money for the silk shirt and the tight leather pants, and a diamond stud in his ear.

"I won't keep you," Kate says.

"She don't mind. She better not. I don't like fetters." It's a new word to him. From the woman. *I'm not trying to keep you in fetters, darling. I just want to be with you.*

"See, I'm her man, but I ain't. You know what I mean."

"Dance with me then."

"Can't dance to no mood music."

It isn't a dancing party. It's the boyfriend party. The husband is out of town, and it's girls' night in with their men. Kate is the only white woman there beside the woman who is with Suliman. She's used to it, the black world. A decision was made, and her life turned black.

"Is she your permanent woman, Suliman?"

"She takes good care of me."

"That's nice. It must be her pleasure."

"That's right. It's her pleasure."

"I'm Kate. I'm here with Stephon, the very young man with the light skin. Much too young for me, but I try not to notice. Not noticing gets essential after forty."

"It's been a while since you've seen forty, Miss Kate."

"I hadn't noticed."

"That's good. I like that. A woman with a sharp tongue. Here, let me give you my card."

Fairlane Motel, 23467 Shaefer, Dearborn, Michigan. 313-464-2500. He has scrawled on the bottom: Suliman Al-Rashid.

"Call me, hear? Mornings are good, but not too early."

"You live in a motel?"

"It's temporary. Till I get my studio back. The lady's paying. I'm staying. Unless she puts me out."

*I wouldn't put you out.*

"Are you a photographer?"

"I'm an artist. Only there's money problems. So I ain't got a studio. Well, I got one, only I owe the rent, so the landlord, he locked me out. All my stuff's locked up. Can't get a paint brush out until I come up with the money."

"What about your lady friend?"

"She ain't interested in the artist part."

*Stephon is someone to sleep with, too, but not a responsibility. Just petty cash.*

*She might be putting on her shoes or almost out of the door—she is always out of the door by midnight and home by 12:30—and Stephon would sit up, sleepy, as if he had just thought of it, his need for money.*

"Thought you were staying the night."

"No, baby. You know I can't."

"Nothing to go home to. That's what you tell me."

"You don't want to see my bedtime routine."

"I was thinking to catch a ride to school with you. My car's out of gas."

"Need some money?"

"Couldn't hurt."

*It is never more than twenty dollars, but it always makes a little hole in her pocket. Mend it, she tells herself. Don't think about how it adds up.*

There are candles on the dining room table; all the silverware is out and the good china. The napkins are in the wrong place—under the knife. She wants to move them, but the hostess won't forget it tomorrow.

Tonight they are beautiful, the women she works with every day. Mahogany with pouty lips and wide doe eyes; honey-gold with high cheek bones, curls caught up in a jeweled clip; close-cropped hair on a perfectly shaped head; tight leather suits or beaded dresses that must have been sewn on.

She admires the Economics teacher, who is thick and definitely off the scale of desirable weight. But she shows a lot of flesh, glistening shoulders, rounded arms, and stocky legs. There is barely a dress, but it is white and gauzy. There are gold hoops in her ears.

There was a time when it was enough to be white.

Stephon is leaning over a woman whose cream-colored arms are around his neck. This is a night that Kate is leaving by herself.

There is plenty of food: ham, turkey, dressing oozing butter, greens, potato salad, macaroni and cheese, sweet potato pie. Pot luck. Home made rolls, pound cake, fried chicken, creamed corn.

She doesn't bring a covered dish to the boyfriend party. A bottle of Chivas Regal is her usual contribution. Next year it won't be Stephon—he'll have a new lady—and it's getting harder to rely on the interest of young men. That's who she prefers.

"I can't promise that I'll call," she says to Suliman, slipping the card in her purse. "But I'll keep the number in case I run across someone who could be a patron for you."

"Patron?"

"A sponsor."

"I don't need a sponsor. I need to get my studio back. I don't need to be selling cereal or something like that."

"Someone who is interested in your art, that's what I mean."

"You know, I was making a joke. I am not no stupid Nee-gro. I been around, read some books, and don't need no teacher to be telling me what a sponsor is."

It's a negotiation, making room for possibilities. Kate understands that. People who don't deserve you but want you in the casual way of sex have to diminish you, keep you off balance. And hadn't she been telling that to her students?

"*Girls, what does it mean, 'Keeping your light under a barrel?'*"

"*Don't let people know how smart you are?*"

If it had gone differently with Stephon, she would not consider this Suliman. Two can play. But he is the winner, disappearing upstairs with the light-skinned woman.

# Chapter Two: Phone Call

Kate doesn't like going after a man who can't afford the price of the pillow he sleeps on. That's a call that she can't afford to make. She has already added up and multiplied the grievances of the tens and twenties she has given Stephon.

"Fairlane Motel. May I help you?"

She has to say the name twice because she can barely get it out of her mouth. Suliman Al-Rashid. A room number would have been easier.

He doesn't speak, but she knows he has picked up the phone.

"Suliman, this is Kate. Last night."

"I ain't forgot."

"That's not what I thought. I am identifying myself."

"I only know two women who would be calling."

"Okay, I'm the other one. I only have a minute...."

"Look, I can't talk to you right now. Let me call you back. No, not a good idea, what with these people paying the bill, wondering what the strange phone number is. You'd be in a world of trouble then."

"I would think you'd be the one in a world of trouble."

He laughs. Kate doesn't like the meanness of it, but she can't pay attention to warnings. She goes right past the signs that say, "Danger: Do Not Enter;" "Caution: Potholes Ahead;" "Sharp Curves: Drive Slowly." She maintains the same speed as if speed is the point, and not the destination.

"So you call me later, maybe around dinner time."

"I could meet you for dinner."

"I ain't got a car."

"Not a problem," she says.

She calls from home at six o'clock and then from a drug store on Telegraph and Six Mile Road. She stops counting how many times she has to say, "May I speak to Suliman Al-Rashid, please?"

Suliman answers at seven o'clock. "I was taking a nap, you know. Couldn't hear the phone."

"You must be quite the sound sleeper."

"You're a snappy little woman."

"I consider myself pretty patient."

"I don't mind snappy women. In fact, I like them. Challenging, you know what I mean? You still up for dinner?"

"I could eat."

"Not where I go with those people, now."

"Those people?"

"My lady. You know."

The woman, the wife, the girlfriend are made anonymous and powerful in the plural. *"Hey, baby, they gonna be mad if I come home too late. I don't want them on my case. They gonna pitch a fit if they find out about you."*

But "they" is always one woman.

This Suliman has made her angry. The anger swells in her. When she walks, extending her feet in front of her in the deliberate style of a lady, the way she has taught the girls to walk, she feels this huge weight of anger that she must carry on her small feet. Anger balloons as if it were lifting her off the ground. But Kate is stubborn. Her stubbornness is more powerful than her anger.

# Chapter Three: The Patron

Chung Lee's is a restaurant in Detroit where people won't stare at a black man with a white woman.

"My family used to come here," she says. "My parents and my brother, I mean. I can order for you in case...."

"I been in a Chinese restaurant before. They don't serve no rolls with dinner."

"It's just that I know what's good on the menu."

"Well, you doing the paying, so it's your call. But I don't do shrimp or lobster. Garbage eaters, that's what they are."

"You are making me very uncomfortable, Suliman."

"I don't like to go around searching for words. It ain't important enough, you know what I mean? There's other stuff to think about. So what's your problem? You never been in public with a black man?"

"I am painfully aware of our age difference."

"That was pretty obvious from the get-go."

"I beg your pardon."

"Nothing, it's nothing. It's my mean streak. In case you haven't noticed. That's just how I am when it's so much on my mind. Stuff I have to figure out."

"Can I help?"

"Why would you want to do that?"

"That's how I am."

"You don't got to be sarcastic."

"Suliman, why aren't we getting along?"

"Look, I am sorry. I am one disappointed man. My life has been snatched away from me, and every day when I wake up, I can't figure how to get it back. There ain't no way to come up with the money to get my stuff back. And even if I did, I wouldn't have a place to put it.

"Like my art, you know, it's my life. I see some stuff lying around, you know, string, glass, maybe rocks. When you find a good rock, a whole world runs through it like a river. In a good rock, you get your inspiration, a god-voice telling you what to do. Anything like that ever happen to you?"

The work of hands: it has been so long since she has prepared a meal or set the table for two. Her hands are about nail polish now, drops of red on her fingertips.

"I'm not an artist," she says.

"I see something, on the ground, you know, I pick it up, rub it, crumble it in my hand. Even touch it to my lips, tasting the earth. Art, it comes right up from the earth. Ain't no barriers between a man and his art."

"I could...."

"And now I can't even see my stuff. That guy got it locked up. He says, 'Suliman, you want to look, you got to pay, the same as rent.' Man won't even let me look at my own stuff. I said, 'You got to be kidding.' He don't even know what it feels like. Like death, but he just wants his money."

"How much does he want?"

"Don't play with me. You don't want to help me out for nothin'. Uh-uh, I ain't going that route again. Room and board, ain't that the deal?"

"I could pay a day's rent."

"For what?"

"Your studio. So you can see your work."

"You ain't kidding. No. You got that do-gooder look on your face."

Kate laughs. "You are so mean," she says.

"Then why you find it so funny?"

"Because I know better. I couldn't please you, not even if I bought you a studio. I would always be a woman buying herself a man. Well, that makes sense. Why would I want to please you if I didn't want to please myself? I'm no saint. Definitely not."

"Well, that's good news. So what we going to order? You do the honors."

Kate orders one egg roll, steak kow, and almond boneless chicken from the tattered menu. She should have chosen a nicer restaurant for Suliman, who is wearing a sports coat and slacks. They should have drinks, but there is only tea at Chung Lee's. She has disappointed them both with this restaurant with so few customers and water-stained walls. But Suliman doesn't seem to notice.

"I don't think the landlord—he's a black man, now—will go with the one day rent business. He wants his rent even if it's just for moving out. Thing is, there ain't a better studio around. And I keep it neat. Every day I need to know where everything is. And I don't want to be ruining brushes, letting the paint dry up. No sir, everything got to be cleaned up and in its place.

"I don't need a television. Been looking at television too long and waiting for those people like a little kid, hoping maybe she'll take me to the zoo. But she only wants to make love.

"You know that expression, *It's a dog's life?* Now I see what it means. I'm a dog chained to a little house, waiting for my bowl of food, waiting to get walked.

"So what you thinking now, Miss Kate? 'I got to lose this guy?'"

"No, I'm adding in my head."

"A lot be riding on your careless words."

"How much is the back rent?"

"Five hundred a month. Ain't just that, you know. That's what already happened."

"How many months do you owe?"

"Three."

Five hundred a month, and electricity, heat, water. Food. The budget she has lectured about in Family Life.

*"Girls, your monthly budget is the bottom line. You must know what you have in order to know what you can spend. Some people prefer the envelope system of budgeting. An envelope for the rent money, the food money, the utility bills, entertainment money, but that one is always the empty one."* The girls write: *"entertainment envelope, usually empty."*

*"Of course, people will raid their envelopes for a little bit of fun. Let's say you take some rent money for the movies or for dinner out. There is always the hope that more money will show up and find its way into the rent envelope. You tell me how that can happen. Most people get paid twice a month with no hope of any other money depositing itself into the rent envelope."* The girls write down every word. Dull and dutiful. They will all have envelopes, thanks to her.

*"I favor the envelope budget, as opposed to the written budget. Figures can be juggled. If you are on a tight budget—and let me say that even if you aren't—the envelope works for everyone. You can't go wrong with putting money in envelopes.*

*"People consider it old fashioned, now with the checkbook. In a way that's true. A checkbook must be balanced, and the numbers treated as actual money. What is spent must be subtracted. Subtraction is the key here. It is the end of illusion."* The girls look up, trying to decide if "illusion" is a household term that must be applied to budgets.

*"I mean that once you know what you have, you can't pretend that you have more."*

"What are your other expenses?"

"I didn't come here for no interrogations."

Kate should walk out and leave Suliman with the bill. But she is staying even though she doesn't know what she is getting for her money.

"For example, I need to eat. I need paints. I need materials. You know any black artists? I don't think so. A black man can't even afford to paint unless he got someone paying him to be an artist. Like a foundation. Or when the government gets worried that, hey, look, we are the United States of America with all these Nee-groes and don't any of them know how to paint. We better get these Nee-groes some real paints and some brushes. Don't want them using those little water color kits from K-Mart."

She has to think about envelopes: five hundred dollars a month for basics, but she doesn't know the kind of light he needs. Supplies, she can't calculate, perhaps fifty dollars.

"I make my own brushes," he says. "I am an inventor of making-do with whatever is lying around. Because all I want to do is paint. You understand? That's all. Else I might as well be dead."

"Well," she says, "we can't have that."

"So?"

"The other lady."

"I'll go to the Disappear-o Market."

"I don't know what you mean."

"Just a story from down home. This couple gets up one day and they walking down the road. People ask, where you going, they say, we going to the market. Only there ain't a market, just a gas station that sells canned stuff and some pop. But they walk down that road and no one ever sees them again. No, not one trace. So whenever we talk about those people, kind of old, we say, yeah, Rufus Lee and his woman, Esta, they gone to the Disappear-o Market."

"That's sad."

"Maybe. Or they had some better place to go than where they were. So, tomorrow going to work for you?"

"Tomorrow? Just like that?"

"Just like that. I got my goodbyes to say, only I ain't saying goodbye in words. And when she leaves, I'm ready. You know, a man ain't free if he has too much to carry when he's walking away."

Then he looks at her as if she is his friend. "Not painters though. We can't walk away from our stuff. Never. That's prison and freedom all at the same time."

"Tomorrow then. After work. I have to get to the credit union for the money...."

"It better be a money order or something that looks like real cash. The landlord ain't playing about his money. And remember the money for what already happened. That's for the key to the place. I need me some forward money, too."

The Christmas money and a loan. Enough for the back rent and one month's expenses. Two thousand; no, twenty-five hundred. To be safe. She'll figure out the rest later.

"You want to come by my room?"

"No."

"I'll be waiting, hear, but I ain't burning bridges. So you better make it five o'clock. The lady never stays to five o'clock because she got dinner to make for the children."

"You're going to leave without saying anything to her."

"Suppose you own a pet dog? And he runs away. Maybe you put his bowl out for a few days, ask around. Even put a reward note on a phone pole. 'Little dog lost. Answers to name of Sexy. Contact owner.' After a few days you forget about that little dog because he wasn't nothing but a pet. You get my meaning? But I'll be a gentleman. Tell 'em at the desk, I got me some business. Lady will settle the bill. Like they don't know who's paying for the bed and the four channel TV and the continental breakfast. But, see, I'm not telling nobody nothing until I got my clothes in your car and one foot inside."

"Five o'clock then."

"Miss Kate...."

"Don't call me Miss Kate."

"...you think you might be a little crazy?"

"I'm not going to answer that."

# Chapter Four: Casey

Casey would have died laughing.

She met him in the bar where the Channel Seven news team did their drinking. She was twenty-eight, and time was measured by the pursuit and the acquisition of a man. That was her clock, running down and winding up.

She came looking for Casey, but she waited to tell the bartender that she had lost her car keys when he came down to the bar from the television studio.

"Hey, Casey, can you help this pretty lady out? She can't find her keys." In the dark bar, the light fell on her red hair, and her long legs were extended.

"Casey Hunter at your service and your pleasure."

If he drove her home, it would mean getting a ride to school in the morning and coming for her car in the afternoon. And with a ticket on it since she parked behind the Art Museum. But she had set her sights on Casey Hunter.

She liked the darkness of him and the pale skin. She wondered how such black hair could grow from such white skin. She liked the thickness of him. Not fat, but burly. "I'm a public figure," he said. "Can't get fat." Which didn't keep him from drinking Scotch instead of water.

There were things about Casey Hunter that Kate did not like, but she chose him, and she would stick to him until the event occurred that was the end of them. It wasn't for always. Nothing was for always except marriage, and she would worry about that when marriage became an issue.

"Where's your car?" he asked.

"Behind the Art Museum."

"Do you want to get it now or later?"

"I've lost my keys."

"Now or later."

"Later."

The University Motel was near Grand Boulevard on Second Avenue. It was out of the way for travelers, relying on transients who did not stay the night.

Casey was a regular. He liked the first floor and a far corner room away from the street noise and where he could keep his car out of sight. A big Cadillac, silver-gray and a black leather interior. Not that his wife would go looking for him in the city. She wouldn't look for him if the University Motel were in her backyard. But Casey kept his business out of Sterling Heights.

"You aren't a hooker."

"I teach Family Life Styles. Home Economics is what they used to call it."

"They're changing the breed. You don't look anything like Miss Craig. She taught Domestic Science."

"For all you know, I'm your Miss Craig in wolf's clothing."
"We'll see."

They sat in the room, drinking Scotch from plastic cups. She sat in the chair, her shoes on the floor and her legs curled under her.

"Let down your hair, Colleen," he said.

"No," she said, "not now."

"I can do what I want," he said.

"Then I would walk away from you forever."

"There are veins of gold in your hair," he said. "A dusting of gold on your arms."

"I wore this dress for you," she said. "I wouldn't wear it to school. I would be sent home or asked to wear a sweater. In this heat."

"I'm married," he said.

"We'll work around it."

"Take off your clothes. Let me see. Something for my dreams, Colleen."

The silk panties, the strapless bra lay on the floor. Only the dress skimmed over the naked flesh of her. A plain dress, almost modest, the skirt gathered at the waist, the girlish scoop of the neck.

"I always wear something green," she said. "Even if it's just a scarf."

"My Colleen," he said. The zipper grated, and the dress fell to the floor.

"There are imperfections."

"I don't see them," he said. "There are no imperfections."

# Chapter Five: Freeway Landing

Casey was a reporter for Channel Seven local news at six and eleven. It was his job to shout out the news, to make it jovial and normal or significant or alarming with his voice.

"I'm not loud," he had said. "I have a stentorian voice."

It was the stentorian voice that had gotten Kate's attention.

"Folks, a Cessna two-passenger plane has made a crash landing on the unfinished stretch of Interstate 696 at the proposed Gratiot exit. Your reporter is standing a few feet away from the wreckage of the plane. And I can tell you that there are no casualties. Police are on the scene, and the site of the crash is roped off. This is the first accident on the new freeway, and it will go down in highway history. Tune in to Channel Seven for updates throughout the night."

Casey didn't know that she was the woman out of the range of the cameras, sitting in the dark police car, putting her hair up, half the pins missing, her shoes rough against her feet without the stockings.

The man before Casey had wanted to marry her. Jimmy, a rich, spoiled boy. But marriage wasn't on her agenda. It was conquer and walk away. A woman could do it, too. Walk away from the man, his desire lingering like wisps of fog.

"Marry me," Jimmy said.

It was like a movie, the dark airfield, small planes rising up in sudden bursts, the headlights sweeping over the two of them. Jimmy, too young and not her type, was holding her by the arm, both of them barefoot on the cool grass. She laughed.

"Wives don't do what I do."

"Not here," he said, pulling her to her feet.

He took her for a plane ride. "Put it on automatic pilot," she said, even though she wasn't sure what that meant.

He landed the plane on a closed stretch of freeway. Before the police came, he had pushed her down on the new cement, and she was telling him, yes, she loved him, anything he wanted, her skirt bunched up around her waist, her stockings caught up in the night wind.

His father was a prominent man, and the police were amused. "Hey, fella, couldn't you think of a better place?"

The plane had skidded to the side of the road, crushed against a cement mixing truck. Jimmy was in handcuffs. "We'll call it involuntary sex," the officer said. "I don't want to get into the rape thing with this guy."

She met the policeman a few times in a motel. She liked his devotion to the act of love. When the freeway was completed, a stretch of I-696, she drove over it a few times, wondering if Jimmy was still married.

Casey was Kate's man, the one she could live with. She liked the bulk of him, the heavy legs, the density of muscle under his silky skin. She liked his generosity. He came to the apartment, bringing the brown-wrapped packages of steak and chicken breasts already cut from the bone, wine in brown sleeves, the ten pound sacks of potatoes, the red tomatoes in a thin cellophane bag, the whipped butter and the cream for coffee. She liked the way he filled the rooms.

"Why do you go home on the weekends? Why don't you stay here?"

"It isn't enough," he said. "One place isn't enough for all the people I am."

"What happens when you get home?"

"We argue. There is a lot of shouting. We get drunk. Then we go out. Sunday, that's the day when we know we can't stay together any longer."

She was Casey's five-sevenths of a wife.

There was her private time: between Friday and Saturday nights, the lost day in between, the day that she would find herself half-clothed or wrapped in a sheet or naked, in someone's apartment, or in a motel. Her two-sevenths of a life before Casey came back.

# Chapter Six: Budgeting

She is getting in too deep with this Suliman, but she can't stop herself. She is caught up in the planning. Check bank account, go to credit union, buy a microwave for the studio. She hopes there is a stove and a refrigerator, not a hot plate and food stored on the ledge in winter. Isn't that what artists do?

The absence of Michael, her husband, allows her to make her list at home. She couldn't do it if he were in the house. He knows her; he would hear the pen scratching out the plans, domestic and erotic. The combination of her.

Rent: $500
Electricity/heat: $50 year-round, no AC
Groceries: $100
Paper goods: $15 (laundry detergent?)
Paints, brushes, canvases???
Telephone: $40, one phone, no extension. No phone?
Total: $705

She can't do it without a loan even though Michael is paying his half of the house expenses. The check is always in the cup in the kitchen every month, the cup that says, "Have a Good Morning," his half of the house payment, utilities, and taxes.

At five o'clock, she will wait outside of the Fairlane Motel. Who will care what Kate Mackey Connally does? There is no one to tell her to do anything but what she is about to do. She has complete freedom to take the remnant end of her life and make it into anything she wants.

*She would like to tell someone about Suliman, but another woman would say to her what she doesn't want to hear: our lives are not for destroying but for creating.*

*She could not make that woman understand that when she is with a man—in bed, or at the stove making him coffee or frying an egg, dressing and undressing for him—that is what she knows of creation. That is her way of being.*

*The other woman would say, "When a woman is in her fifties, her body is a vehicle to get her to the places she needs to be, not on stages where men act themselves out."*

"That's where I want to be," Kate would say, "on that stage. Life is nothing without a man, without the act of sex, my preference, a harsh and brutal plunging, but time enough for me to slow it down, wear it to a silken finish. That is creation too."

She goes to Fairlane Mall. It is in Dearborn, near the motel. She can no longer figure and refigure the costs of Suliman.

The two thousand dollars is in an envelope marked "debt." She has written a check at the credit union, her last instant loan. The loan board does not have to decide. *Should we let this teacher have two thousand dollars so that she can finance a young black man about whom she knows absolutely nothing, has never even kissed him or touched his hand, and he will be doing her a favor, no matter what he does for her because isn't the game over, look at her birth date, 1949.*

Where did the money go? Casey had taken care of her expenses until he got sick, but where did her salary go? Then she lived on her own, the best time of her life because Casey was dying and yes, she felt horrible, but she was free, and every day was like being in a garden where she could pick anything she wanted. Saturdays looking for an antique show. Or going to Windsor and smuggling in a pair of shoes for the thrill of flirting with the customs officer so that he never would ask: "What do you have in the trunk of your car, fire arms, alcohol, drugs?" And the men. What is your pleasure? It will be mine.

She once enjoyed shopping in the big malls, but now she has a careful clothing budget that only allows for a small fling, a sweater, a bracelet, a nightgown.

*"Rule, girls. No expenditure over $100 without a family conference. You and your husband—these days she would have to say partner, fiancé, significant other—must discuss the purchase of a major item, a couch, television, suit, winter coat. Try to shop at the end of the season. Being careless with money brings nothing but trouble. Don't kid yourself. The mismanagement of money can break a marriage. You only have two choices: go to work or practice thrift."*

Thrift is outside of Kate's control. Sometimes it breaks her heart when her money flies out of her hands. She can't bear thinking that someone is taking it from her. She prefers the belief that money has its own impetus.

It never works when you try to take from men. They aren't in it to be taken. They are renting. What they pay is always on the low side, always to their advantage. Even when she isn't interested, when she doesn't care if the man walks out the door or takes her out to dinner, what he will give is the least he can afford.

But the men aren't renting any longer. Kate is not a young woman. In her efforts to please a man for the short-term, sometimes she doesn't make the grade. The failures make her angry, only the feeling is more like tears and despair. She never knew anger could be like that, so full of pain.

What is she supposed to do, sit at home and crochet? Look at television? No. Without sex there isn't anything. No one could tell her that there is anything without a man. There is not one thing that is more important than having a man in her bed.

So it is Suliman by default because he is the last stop. And he will take some real thinking. He will be a real problem.

She gets a cup of coffee at the mall because she has given herself too much time for waiting. She looks at the women, some with daughters, others with friends, pulling aside garments, unfolding blouses on the sale racks, looking through the socks and the handbags, getting a free makeover. It can't be amusement; it can't be pleasure.

Pleasure was her daughter, Shannon, taking a nap, and the precious hour is for ironing the pink and white pinafore that Shannon will wear in the afternoon. Pleasure was her husband, Michael, reaching for detergent or tomato sauce in the supermarket while she recited from the list prepared according to familiar aisles. Pleasure was the squeak of rubber gloves as she wrung out the cloth for cleaning the sinks and bathtub, the smell of Clorox and lemon-scented Pledge and Easy-Wax on the kitchen floor.

She had believed that these pleasures would endure forever, repeating themselves in daily predictability like the lessons plans she uses each year, the foolproof plan for family living.

*"Girls, the rules are always the same. There must be order, cleanliness, budgeting, healthy food, and exercise. Baths and naps and clothes folded when they come out of the dryer. Don't let the ironing build up. Take it a garment at a time. Foolproof. Order is foolproof."*

But you can't order chaos, not ordinarily. But these aren't ordinary times. Order, ordinary, well, of course, they would go together. They have gone together.

# Chapter Seven: Leaving Dearborn

It's cold, but she walks the long way to her car at the edge of the mall parking lot. She is five minutes from the motel. Perhaps Suliman is alone. She can knock on the door, say something like "Housekeeping" or "Did you call the desk, sir, for more towels?" And if he says, "I'm busy," then she will go back to her car. She will park it somewhere where it can't be seen. It is better to wait there where waiting is a real thing, not a pretense that she is interested in the counters and the racks, the coats at half off or the skirts stuffed back among the wrong sizes.

The motel parking lot is empty. He is probably looking at television or waiting for the same creeping hours to go by.

She knocks. There is silence. She knocks again. "Yeah? Who is it?" "Me," she says; "it's me."

He is glad to see her even though he is scowling. He has been sleeping.

"I ain't even ready," he says, "but, hey, getting ready don't take much time." He takes a towel and spreads it on the bed. "I figure with all this rent they owe me some mo-mentos of the Fairlane Motel." He piles underwear in the center of the towel and ties it corner to corner.

"We're just going to pile the hanging clothes in the trunk, right?" He empties the trash basket and takes the liner for his shoes and his bathroom kit.

"So let's hit the road. I am out of here."

She watches him through the rearview mirror, shaking out the garments and placing them in the trunk of the car. How handsome he is when he is not trying to be casual and diffident. The only power he has is turning the blank face of sexuality toward the women, maybe men, too, just so that he can get by.

"Look at that. Grown man with no suitcase. All I need is a stick, and I'm like one of them tramps in the movies."

"It's okay," she says, "you didn't know you would be leaving."

"Neither did the other people. Tell the truth, I feel a little bad. Like she isn't a real bad person, but she likes her money's worth, you know what I'm saying? I asked her—I got to start speaking more proper now that I'm not a house pet—'Please, give me the money going for this room, so's I can be with my stuff, my art. Everything else will be the same between us. Fact is, it will be better.' No way. I see where she was coming from, though. This way she's got the key, she's got the credit card, she's got the power. 'You'd lock me out when you get tired of me,' she said. Doing it her way, I had no choices but to be looking at cartoons until she decided to drop by.

"Man, I wouldn't want to be a woman if that is their deal. Hey, look, I didn't tell you where to go. West side of Woodward, you know, near the 94 expressway."

Suliman is restless, anxious. Staying too long in one place makes you afraid to leave. Didn't she know that?

"Linda, that's her name, she didn't like driving around Detroit with her big Lincoln. You know that party? I had to beg her to let me out of the motel. 'It might be a bad neighborhood,' she said. You can't get Ford Motor Company, Dearborn, aren't-we-top-of-the-line people to go into The Ghetto unless you got a gun to their heads. I love the way they say it, like in capital letters, THE GHETTO. Like it ain't houses and sidewalks same as everywhere else in the world. Man, people do amaze me, how their houses got to be better and their sidewalks safer even though we be living five minutes away.

"Been so long, I don't even know how to get back home in a car. Guess you should take Michigan Avenue. Wouldn't mind driving this old car myself. Well, not right now, but one day, you know. My license's kind of old, and I wouldn't want you getting into trouble over me.

"Listen to me talking like I just got out of jail. Fact of the matter, I have been in jail. But that's a whole different story.

"Tell you this, I definitely do not want to be seeing Linda again any time soon. Not only is she going to blow sky high when she comes strolling in Monday or whenever she gets the chance, she'll be looking for blood. That is not one forgiving woman, but butter don't melt in her mouth when she's calling home and talking to her husband or one of her kids. 'Honey, I didn't notice the time, and here I am in Bloomfield Hills, and it's the height of traffic. I will be home in a jiffy, but order out, pizza is fine.' Whatever. Then she wants some more of what I been giving her. Some days it ain't easy. Some days it takes real concentration to jump through Miss Linda's hoops.

"Once, one little time, I'm not at the motel when she gets there. When I come back, I can't get in the room. Go to the desk, ask what's going on, and they say the lady ain't paying the rent any more. So I'm out on the street, which is okay for a couple of days, like it wasn't winter. But it ain't Hawaii either, so I can't sleep on the beach and crack open a cocoanut. Then I call her and I have to beg—it's pitiful—so that I can have a bed to sleep in and something to eat. Not to mention that the purse strings got tighter.

"The city's looking good. Man, I love this place. A painter's delight. Someone called it that, some white dude, only he was taking photographs of the falling down, beautiful city and painting at home. 'Doom City, Dead City,' he said, 'and I am not taking any chances out there with my sketch pad.' He was missing something even though he got down the way things looked. But he didn't get how things felt.

"It's something else, shadow and flame. Polluted sunsets and dirty snow, dogs in the garbage, and all the houses leaning over. Doesn't make a difference. The city got this way, and all the hoping in the world, well, it don't change anything. You got to see the beauty. Hey, you got to turn at the next street. I'm talking too much and not paying attention to the road."

The streetlight at the corner of Aurelia is burnt out. Kate sees only shadows of houses and lights flickering in windows, as faint as candles.

"Well, here we are. Home. I'm telling you, my whole life I will never forget how I feel right now."

Kate cannot rely on her voice to ask Suliman what he feels. She will be betrayed by the cajoling voice of a woman wanting to please but never being able to please him as much as the opening of the door to his home.

"But this ain't the time to talk about it," he said. "I'm finding that guy and paying him. I mean that's the deal, isn't it? Paying him backwards and forwards a little bit. Till I get on my feet."

Kate hands him the envelope. He says, "This isn't payment, not like Linda, right? This is an act of friendship. The rest comes by itself. I don't want to be a pet, not any more."

"I'll be your sponsor."

"Not to be mean, Miss Kate, but women use all kind of words when all they mean is sex. Right now, you understand, I'm feeling dirty. Linda made me feel dirty. So maybe we can hold back a little, you know what I'm saying?"

"Don't concern yourself about it, Suliman."

"Hey, not like you ain't a great looking woman for your age. And I am a fool for not wanting to stretch out with you just for the pure pleasure of it. But you'd be a fool, too, if you take it as payment."

She is playing the game with a master. She wants to snatch the envelope from him, the $2000 scraped and borrowed and taken from those other payment envelopes, not that she keeps them anywhere except in her head. So much for this, so much for that. So much to buy a foot in the door with a man whose real name she doesn't even know.

He is so clever, Suliman, Solomon, whoever he wants to be, but she knows some games herself. It will be her serve, but right now the ball is in his court.

"The ball is in your court."

"I'm supposed to know what that means, like I been playing games instead of losing who I am."

"All right then, who are you? I don't even know your real name, the one on your license. A patron should know these things."

He is sullen again. "I ain't got a license right now. I think I told you that."

"Of course, you'll renew it as soon as you have a permanent address."

"Gary Johnson. But don't be calling me that. So now you got your way."

"Suliman, I don't even know what my way is. You have two thousand of my dollars in your hand, and I don't remember making a contract. I gave you money to get your life back, and somewhere along the very short ride we have been on, you have decided that you can treat me any way you want, and I know why. Because I am not young. I am old. I am fifty-eight years old, and I haven't even asked you how old you are. Thirty-two, thirty-five.

It doesn't matter because the Grand Canyon is sitting here right between us, and it is made up of years.

"Thirty-seven. And I am not proud to be begging from white women."

"I don't blame you. Really. You should find the man who has the key to your studio and give him what you owe him and the next month's rent. I am going to sit in the car and wait. To make sure it is all right, because if it isn't, you can still go back to the motel and pretend you never left."

"One thing is for sure, I ain't going back to the motel. Sleep in the street first."

"I don't think that is true."

"Okay, we won't play. I'm going to find Reginald. Then I am going in the house that I've been locked out of so long that I don't even know what's in it any more. I am going to take you on a tour of the great works of Suliman Al-Rashid because you're the sponsor. And I hope you will consider being my friend. I haven't treated you right, and you didn't ask one thing of me. I jumped to my conclusions, and I insulted you, too. No excuse for that."

"You should find your landlord."

"Don't go anywhere. You got my stuff."

Kate shouldn't be here, but it doesn't matter any more where she is. No one is looking for her; no one is waiting for her.

She waits for Suliman to come running back to the car with a tall man with parchment-colored skin. "This is Reginald, and we settled up with each other," he says, opening the car door and taking out the wrapped towels. "Only thing is he turned the heat down real low, and...."

"Thing is, Suliman," Reginald says, "I need a guarantee from the lady that I don't have to be putting you out again. Is that right, Miss? Do I have a verbal guarantee that I am not wasting my time with Suliman the artist? Because I can rent this place tomorrow for maybe twice what is owed me for what I am giving. And heat costing what it do, I don't need to be running up no bill if I got to shut it right down again in thirty days."

"You don't have any worries, Mister...."

"Calvert. The name you can write on the check, Mr. Reginald Calvert."

"I'll remember."

"And I won't be appreciating any temporary checks like yesterday you opened a bank account cause you're new in town. No way. I got to have cash or a check with all the vital statistics on it, name, address, city and state. Phone number got to be good in case Suliman is hard to find, him being a young buck and all. No telling what he do when folks ain't looking."

"No need to be talking that way to the lady, Reginald. You got your money, so our business for the day is over."

"It got to be like clockwork, Suliman. The rent and all. Good night to you, Miss. I know you be taking care of the economic end of it, so I'm depending on you." Reginald rushes away and disappears into a house where only one light glows in the window.

"Even though it's cold, come on in, look around," Suliman says.

"I can come back another time."

"Tomorrow, hear. Say, can you flip the trunk? I got my clothes in there."

She can go to another mall, maybe Twelve Oaks this time. Or a restaurant. A woman eating alone, the early bird special before six o'clock. The couples would come in, seniors mostly, looking at her, looking at each other, glad that there were two of them. She can go to a bar, but time doesn't seem to move in a bar. And time has to move. She has to get to midnight every night in some place that isn't home.

"Why don't you take in your clothes and give the place a chance to warm up. We could go to eat."

He hesitates; he wants to be alone with what he has been dreaming of: dried paint on the floor, the stacked canvases, the single bed somewhere out of sight, a two burner stove, the stained glass of the windows that looked black on the outside, his private Tahiti.

"Okay," he says. "I know a place right around here. Nice little place, Polish food. Been a while. We can celebrate cause this is my lucky day."

Then it is okay. There is somewhere to go and after that, well, they can work it out. There will be a schedule. She will let him know that she won't go home at night before Michael. They can talk about the rent, the food, and the exchange would be time for money. Cards on the table. That's what they had to do, put their cards on the table. But not about the sex.

There are two other couples in the restaurant.

"It's not a fancy place," Suliman says.

There are five tables in the restaurant and four wooden chairs at each table. There are no tablecloths, and the paper napkins are rolled like flowers in a jar. The menu is written on a blackboard, and some items have been erased.

It doesn't matter because she doesn't have to go home. She is going to string this out as long as she can so that she gets home later than Michael. *It doesn't matter where I go, Michael, as long as I'm not there. Those are the rules.*

"They got really good bread here"

"It's interesting about bread. It depends upon the availability of fuel. The Chinese, for example, don't serve bread with their meals. Everything has to be cooked quickly because of the shortage of fuel. And tortillas...."

"I keep forgetting that you're a school teacher."

"I learned that on television."

"I mean to get a TV now that the motel is, you know, behind me. Not saying that I couldn't paint night and day, but a man needs a break every now and again. But, hey, until it works out, I can just go down to the corner and drink a slow beer and look at some programs."

"But getting back to painting, isn't that the most important thing?"

"Hey, there ain't no life without my work."

"I'd like to see your work."

"No doubt about it, you being the sponsor now."

"No, not like that. I want to know the kind of person you are."

"I don't mean to speak out of turn, but it don't matter what kind of person I am. You want somewhere to hang. Okay, you got a deal. Tomorrow you get a key made, and how do they say it, 'Mi casa, su casa.'"

"Something like that."

"You know, Kate, I ain't a stranger to being lonely. I can spot it. When I saw you at the party, I was thinking to myself, 'What is this lady doing here?' Linda, she pitched a fit when I told her I wanted to go to the boyfriend party. My cousin—it's her house—tells me to bring my woman, no one cares about who you bring to the boyfriend party. I tell her, Linda, that I want to get out of the cage, and she's thinking I'm about to fly the coop. Like I had somewhere to go. But ain't it all play acting?

"It didn't make sense, you being there with that joker. Him not even knowing he's lower than the street. And I know right on the spot that you are one lonely lady even though I know you come from a nice home and a whole different world. Far as I'm concerned the only reason you're at the boyfriend party is to pass the time. Ain't I right?"

"Yes."

"Just checking to see if my instincts are still good. Let's read the blackboard and order us a celebration dinner. Kielbasa and the sauerkraut looking good to me. How about you."

"Pierogi," Kate says. "It's been a long time since I have eaten pierogis."

# Chapter Eight: Cleaning Supplies

Suliman is standing in the door of the dark, narrow house on a corner where the trees are struggling to stay alive because it is all pavement. But it is winter. It must be pretty in springtime, looking out of the high windows on the third floor, and a good place for painting with all the light. All that she can see behind him are opened cartons and a rough, brick floor.

"You know, I need to check the place out, maybe get back to Reginald. See if he messed with my stuff." Reginald lived on Aurelia, too. Cross street, I-94 service drive. Suliman's house is on the corner. 5746 Aurelia. She won't forget.

"And you don't want to be coming in because I can see right now, I got a lot of cleaning up to do before I entertain." He is trying to look down the dark street for Reginald without leaving the doorway.

"I can handle a mess. Tomorrow, I am going to...."

"Move right in, ain't that it?"

"I thought I'd help with the cleaning."

"From what I see here, it's more like hauling and pitching. Man been storing his stuff in here. Stacked my paintings up against the wall, probably before they got dry. Well, he is getting a bill for storage from me. But this ain't your problem. You done enough."

"In the morning I can help you out."

"That'd be good."

"I should go home," she says, "but if you need anything tonight...."

"This day's been too long already, like a day with a thousand hours."

"Tomorrow?"

"Sure, tomorrow's going to be fine between you and me."

"Not too soon?"

"It's another day, ain't it?"

"Yes. Tomorrow. I'll see you tomorrow."

Driving home, Kate thinks about Windex or ammonia. Or maybe both. First, the ammonia and then a finishing rub with Windex. Pine Sol, Lysol Toilet Bowl Cleaner, and a brush. Comet with bleach. A hard scrubbing brush. Disposable cloths. She doesn't want to ruin good rags.

*"You would be so surprised, girls, about the importance of rags. The sources are infinite." The girls look up from their note taking. Infinite. They are wondering how to spell it and if it is the same word used for the power of God. "For example, you can use old washcloths although their use is limited. I wouldn't dust with a washcloth because it would absorb too much of the Pledge or whatever brand you choose for dusting. When you dust, it is more important that the product is absorbed by the wood than the cloth. That's the point, isn't it, of dusting? To oil the surfaces while you are eliminating the tiny motes of dust that fall each minute, spoiling the look of your living room or dining room."*

Motes of dust have been falling in the streams of the motionless air of the closed-up, old house. They have been seeping up from the floorboards, from the dampness of the basement, drying and turning to dust. Suliman will sleep on layers of dust. Does he mind? The way she does?

Kate drives into the garage at ten thirty. It's as late as she can manage. She doesn't know if Suliman has a blanket or a pillow. There is nothing she can do about it. Not tonight. Her face is melting as if it were wax.

She cannot sleep. She thinks of getting up at four in the morning and going to Meijer's for cleaning products. She can't wait to be the cleaning woman for a man with dreadlocks and a bad temper. But Michael is in the house, and she won't have him filing away any evidence against her: the splinters of light that creep out under the bathroom door, the splash of water against the shower wall, the whisper of her feet on the carpet, the snapping shut of the closet door, and the cranking up of the garage door, the slight whine of the ignition when she starts up her car. She doesn't get up, but she dreams herself in the aisles of the all-night superstore, in the aisles of bleaches, cleansers; of Lysol, Windex, Pledge, Murphy's Oil Soap; of mops and brooms and toilet bowl brushes; buckets for washing and for rinsing.

*"Don't believe for a minute, girls, that a quick mopping of the kitchen and the bathroom floors means that you have done a proper cleaning. No, our grandmothers were right. Get down on your knees with the old-fashioned scrub brush and not one, but two buckets. The whole kit and caboodle. Wash and rinse, wash and rinse. There are products out there, kneeling pads that you can strap to your legs to protect your knees. But in a pinch folding a bath towel into a cushion and moving it along with you as you scrub works just as well. And then throw those rags into the washing machine, with a lot of bleach, of course."*

The girls laugh when she says "caboodle." It is an old word, one that they have probably not heard. She hadn't meant to say it, not that or the part about grandmothers because isn't she almost old enough to be a grandmother to the girls she instructs in a way of life she doubts they will pursue.

# Chapter Nine: Michael

She has fallen asleep in the aisles of detergents and kitchen supplies. It is Saturday, Michael's day to sleep, and the house is heavy with him. She knows from long memory the deep sighs of his sleeping, the little-boy look of him.

Today she is washing her hair and wrapping it in a heavy towel until it is dry enough to brush out over her shoulders. She will take time to shave her legs and soak in the bath.

*"Girls, when it comes to personal beauty care, the stars knew best. For instance, Lana Turner"*—the girls look at her with blank faces—*"Lana Turner, who could afford the most expensive body oils in the world, used sesame oil on her face and her famous movie star body. You might be wondering if she smelled like sesame chicken or egg fu yung, but that is what is so good about sesame oil. It is light and has no smell once the skin absorbs it.*

*"Doris Day, a popular singing star, covered her body with Vaseline and wrapped herself in a sheet once a month for an entire night. That was her special beauty treatment, common Vaseline."*

She is going to look into the mirror and see an old woman. But as the steam clears from the bathroom mirror, she sees a radiance she doesn't expect. She looks so young. She is fooling herself, of course. She is seeing what she wants to see.

What Kate believes, more than the superiority of old diapers as the ultimate household rag or of vinegar as the cheapest and most effective household cleaner, is that the sexual act—or the anticipation of it—is an act of renewal. Lovemaking keeps a woman young.

She blames herself for Michael's turning away from her in bed; the secrets that knocked and rattled at their marriage, echoes of her secrets, the shadow-presence of her ghosts. Michael had none. He had acknowledged his simple failures, the three divorces, the impossible child support, the jobs he had lost. The ghosts that paced the rooms and sulked in the dark corners of the kitchen were Kate's.

She didn't believe that anyone had come forward and said to him, "Say, aren't you married to Kate Mackey? She has been around a few blocks in her day and not particular about the neighborhood."

She is the one who has betrayed herself: she is too practiced in bed and not patient enough to wait for the tentative turning of her husband, who isn't interested as much in sex as he is in the house and the clean sheets and the 5:30 dinners.

She was tyrannical in her marriage, following the lessons of her Marriage and Family Living class. She was Wife. And Michael went along with it. For a while. The shopping together, doing the laundry, the folding, the two of them in the kitchen, filling bowls with sour cream dip and cutting broccoli flowerets and carrot sticks for Friday night drinks. He drives her to school so that they can share the time together. A schedule, her schedule.

*"A good marriage integrates sex into the daily routine, girls. It isn't about you. It's about keeping him happy."*

Their marriage has become the art of avoiding one another, an act of division: I take the living room, you get the family room. I sleep in the master bedroom; you sleep in Shannon's room.

She always knows when he is at home; the house whispers of him. Sometimes she can't sleep until she hears the murmur of the television from the family room, a shiver through the pipes when he flushes the toilet, his careful sliding through the rooms when he is not sure where she is.

She wants to isolate a time when it went wrong. She is a detective of each day, turning over an event as if it were a trail with particular markings that she could interpret. The day she washed his white shirts with a pair of blue socks that ran, and he was so angry. It could be that. The pot roast burned because they stayed too long at Sears, and there was smoke damage all over the kitchen. It took them half a day to scrub it down, and then they had to eat at McDonald's. No, he was just annoyed. He had wanted to stay at home, but she had insisted that they go together.

She can't say how long it has been since they have spoken. Maybe she doesn't want to know because years are like tape measures. They don't lie. They tell what size you are, and sometimes you don't want to know what it is.

She didn't see it coming because she was busy. She was the breadwinner, the bill payer, the decorator, the laundress, the chef, and yes, finally, the mother. Her entire life had been heading toward these roles, the ones she created every semester for the girls.

She had been painting a mural of home, and the passing of time was marked by the changing colors of the rooms, the curtains replaced with draperies, the draperies giving way to horizontal blinds. The newly upholstered couch, giving the room a whole new look, the antiqued dining room table that took so long to strip and stain and then to distress, just enough to make it interesting. Shannon's crib, her youth bed, the four-poster, then the closed door.

Michael had started a new PR job with the city of Southfield, no fixed hours, and that meant dinners covered with a napkin, finally using the Christmas money for a microwave, and then the waste.

There was so much to do, and there was worry, a gathering of quicksand beneath the new tiles in the kitchen—so expensive to replace. Worry can keep you busy in ways that are exhausting.

She worried about the waste of food.

*"There is no excuse, girls, to turn good food into garbage."* She throws up her hands in alarm at the waste of meat, mashed potatoes left in the pot, a head of lettuce turning brown. *"What we throw in the garbage pail and down the disposal*

*was once something we pondered over at the vegetable bins in the supermarket, at the meat counter, in the bakery section. We couldn't make do without it. So how did it get to be garbage? We didn't treat it correctly. We didn't think ahead.*

*"Wouldn't you be embarrassed if you had guests and you didn't have enough food to go around? Of course. You plan to have enough for as many people as you had invited. In order to prevent perfectly good food from becoming garbage, you have to plan in reverse. You cut a chicken in parts and use only what you need. You eliminate the extra starch, the rice or the pasta. You keep it simple: meat loaf and potatoes, hot dogs and beans, pork chops and apples. Or a nice stew with lots of vegetables and little chunks of meat. What you don't use, you freeze.*

*"If you wait too long, if you leave that food in the oven, or if you zap it in the microwave one time too many because someone is late, someone didn't make it to dinner, then you are stuck with garbage."*

She stopped buying, and she stopped cooking. She ate cereal or a peanut butter sandwich. By then Shannon only wanted pizza. If he had asked her why there was no dinner when he came home from the meetings or from the mayor's cocktail parties where there was too much to drink and not enough to eat, she would have told him that she couldn't turn food into garbage. One day he said it for her.

"This is all garbage," he said, waving his hand around. She should have asked if they both shared the definition of garbage. That might have helped, knowing if they were talking about the same thing when they said the word, garbage.

She knew Michael in bed, his body turning toward her even when he didn't move. He is so quiet in the dark as if he is holding his breath in anticipation of the sliding of her leg against his, her heat meeting his coolness. She lifts the edge of her nightgown as if it were the corner of a tablecloth being turned back to show the polish and the grain of the wood. The nightly invitation is hers to make.

One night he turns away. You don't ask questions when it happens once. You hold your tongue, touch the shoulder that has been turned away from you, the back that rises like a ridge. You show sympathy for a bad day, things on his mind, and aching muscles from that day when he had played eighteen holes of golf.

It is never again. She waits and waits, and then it occurs to her: she will never again feel his skin against hers.

He does not forgive Kate for making him a father one more time.

"I don't have room for this," he shouts at her. "There isn't room enough in me. Don't you understand?"

"No room?" she asks. "For this pathetic excuse of a life?"

He loves Shannon as if she were the prize among his many children, the one that finally pleases him, and the one he could finally give something to even if he was a man who always found himself with nothing to give. But he hates Kate equally.

"For yourself," he tells her. "I don't like you for yourself." He says more, but she won't listen.

She shouts, "How dare you, how dare you? After all I have done."

"Iron maiden," he says. She looks at him, bewildered. Isn't that an instrument of torture? She starts to cry, but he can't stop. "Would you like to be called cookie cutter rather than 'iron maiden'? A nice harmless cookie cutter? It's all the same. The shape you want comes out. The shape you want."

## Chapter Ten: Saturday Night

Margaret. Her mother's name is Margaret. The people she went to live with might have called her Margarita or maybe Grandma. It was the senior citizen center in Los Angeles. David, her brother, had gone looking for her a few months after Margaret had packed two suitcases and walked out of the door.

"She's living in a boarding house. With a family of illegal immigrants. As if she's been there forever."

"Leave it alone," she told her brother. "It's her choice."

"I'm not paying for my mother to live in a slum."

"I'll sell the house," Kate said.

Selling the house meant sorting through the closets, the drawers, the attic, and the basement. It meant deciding what to save, what to sell, what to give to Salvation Army and Purple Heart, what to leave at the curb for the "salvagers," the people who came by late at night before pickup day. It meant remembering.

"Treasures can't be purchased," her father would say. He liked it spare, no clutter. "The less the better," he would say, as if he had been planning to leave all along.

On weeknights he never came home. Margaret would always prepare enough food for him and set his place. Kate believed that he ate his dinner at a Coney Island or at Cunningham's, breakfast served all day. Perhaps he had soup and a sandwich or bacon and eggs. If he happened to be downtown, he might have roast beef and mashed potatoes in a cafeteria.

Now she knows better. All those years while his plate, his cup, his glass, his fork, his knife, his paper napkin were arranged at his place at the table, he was eating in another house where a woman brought a tuna fish casserole to the table or broiled meat and baked potatoes. They drank beer or wine. Perhaps she baked an upside down cake or brownies. Her father drank his tea and looked at television among the bric-a-brac of another house whose clutter and accumulations were charming to him.

"Did dad ever come home to dinner during the week?" she asks her brother when they are looking for Margaret in Tijuana, where she had moved with the Mexican family. *We took Grandma with us, she was so lonely. It seemed the right thing to do. We don't need any money. The social security is enough.*

"Well, did he? I can't remember."

"Not as far as I know," David says. "Except for Saturday night and Sunday lunch."

On Saturday night they went out to dinner at Victor Lim's. Margaret wore her print dress with big flowers. She fixed her hair so that it fell across her brow, "just like Veronica Lake." She wore a little hat. David, their father, took her arm when they walked from the car to the restaurant. He read the menu out loud, but the choices were always the same: steak kow and almond boneless chicken.

If she had been sitting at another table, Kate would have said, "What a nice family. The mother is so pretty and adoring. The father beams at his children, who are hoping for an extra egg roll so that they won't have to share."

Margaret loved egg rolls, but only two came with dinner. "Two dinners are enough for a family," her father said, "with all the rice and two bowls of soup." Margaret took the soup. Kate doesn't remember a time when her mother ever ate an egg roll, but after her father left, there were no Saturday night dinners or Sunday lunches or places set at the table during the week.

Kate does not eat egg rolls. "You don't know what is in them," she says. After she is married, she is never one to suggest Chinese food for the family.

David, the father, always left after Sunday lunch. The key turned in the lock on the next Saturday at five o'clock. If it were any later, Margaret would be alarmed. Something had gone wrong. An accident, a mugger, a blow on the head. Murder on another street. The possibility of murder echoed in the house until the key was turned in the lock, the closet door was opened in the hall if it was winter, and the coat was put away. The steps in the hall would give beneath his weight. He was a short man and heavy, and pretty Margaret had once been a prize for him because he was not handsome or rich.

There had been no murder. They can go to Victor Lim's.

When he had decided to leave the family, Kate's father came to the house during the week. Kate came to the door when she saw the car pull up. A woman was sitting in the passenger seat.

"Hi, dad."
"Katey."
"Is there something…?"
"I'm divorcing your mother."
"I'm not going to be the one to tell her."
"No need. I thought you should know. And David."
"Are you divorcing us, too?"
"No need to say that, Katey."
"No?"
"You will always be my girl."

# Chapter Eleven: Rules One through Eight

Kate had not believed her father. In fact, she believed very little of what people told her. She did believe in her set of rules or precautionary measures, compiled over time and tested against failure.

Rule number one: Do not set your sights on an unattached man. The ball is in his court and not in yours. Kate does not play tennis, but she has heard the saying often enough: the ball is in your court.

Rule number two: Go home at the end of the night even if it is closer to morning. A man should be left alone in his bed or the bed that has been rented. He will feel hostile to the woman who has (not) been satisfied, who might want breakfast, who does not look as attractive in the morning.

Rule number three: Keep out of harsh lights, a rule that Kate thought of moving up to number one when she turned forty.

Rule number four: Arrive in your own car.

Rule number five: Consummation is the most important element in trafficking with men. Sex is the payment.

Rule number six: Nothing should get in the way of the consummation.

Rule number seven: Find the good in the adulterous relationship. Kate considers moving this rule to first place and the unattached-man rule to second place, but she doesn't want to lose sight of her goal, which is not to be trapped in a marriage. When she attends bridal showers, and the bride-to-be holds up a saucepan as if she had been given a treasure, Kate sees the bride-to-be drowning, weighted down with pots and potato mashers and electric can openers.

Rule number eight: Do not visit your married friends. You might be tempted to seduce the husband. At the very least, the visit will be uncomfortable.

Kate does not have women friends. She doesn't want competition, but it isn't that either. It's intimacy she doesn't want. She is friendly, and there is always a table where she is welcome to sit in the teacher's lunchroom, but she rarely goes to lunch. Talking leads to revealing things. It is the revealing of self that Kate avoids, even to herself. The Rules are as far she is going. Knowing what she wants is comparable to knowing who she is.

# Chapter Twelve: Rule Number Nine

Rule number nine: Being sexy is not about being naked. It is an attitude that transcends clothing. Clothing should never speak for you or announce your intentions. The appearance of modesty is more useful than the appearance of availability.

Rule number nine was forced on Kate.

She is fifteen or sixteen and riding the bus home from downtown, the Dexter-to-Outer Drive bus. The green Hudson's bag is at her feet, and her new black leatherette purse is on her lap. It is hot, summer, and she is wearing a sleeveless sundress. It is yellow.

A man is approaching, and Kate gathers up the full skirt of the sundress because it is spread out on the seat next to her. It is a courtesy, not an invitation.

The windows of the bus are open, and it is noisy with the sounds of the street and the laboring engine of the bus. She doesn't hear what he is saying at first. He says it again: *I want to fall into you like rain.* What, she says, what? He says, *I want to cover you with all the seasons, snow on your arms, leaves on your thighs, petals where you blossom.*

Kate reaches for the cord to signal a stop even though she is more than a mile from her corner. *Pull the cord,* he says, his voice part of the wind, the roar of the street, *and I will lift your burning hair and cool the hot nape of your neck with my tongue.* "Mister," she says, but it is only a whisper. She should shout, but what can she say? "This man is saying things to me that I do not understand." The woman across the aisle reading a magazine would say, "What do you expect when you wear a dress without sleeves." The man in front of her would say, "You were asking for it."

The man does not touch her, and he does not speak to her again. He is smiling, not at her but at some thought that has swept across him, something that has nothing to do with her.

When she sees the familiar drugstore on the corner, she pulls the cord. "Excuse me," she says, clutching her packages in front of her, her leatherette purse. "Excuse me." He moves his legs aside and lets her pass. There is nothing, not even recognition.

The sundress is shoved to the back of the closet. She means to wear it again. She doesn't, and she can't.

Rule number ten: Accept the blame for whatever happens. It will always be your fault.

# Chapter Thirteen: Covering Up

Sometimes Kate teaches clothing. She prefers it to the foods classes because it is more orderly, and the girls are interested, if not enthusiastic, about making their own clothes.

"*Your basic skirt is the easiest to run up,*" she tells the girls, "*for your first project. Choose a nice, solid color. We can worry about matching patterns later in the semester.*"

Kate keeps the pattern books at her desk. She insists on choosing the correct skirt or blouse for each girl. It is the first step in creating the proper wardrobe. She calls each girl up to her desk in alphabetical order and turns the pages of the Butterick Pattern book.

She never sews clothes for herself. She shops at Penney's and Marshall's because she knows that she will find clothing that will serve her purpose, which is to cover her body. If it would not attract too much attention, she would wear a head covering like Arab women wear or the veil that a widow wears standing over a coffin.

The widow takes off the veil the moment she gets home. "I couldn't see a thing. Who was there?"

What is grief anyway but feeling sorry for yourself that you have to start everything all over again to regain what you had worked so hard for? A man who belonged to you, a house with two floors, carpeting, and a good quality linoleum. (She would have to remind the girls during the Home Decorating unit not to stint on linoleum. "*Don't think of it as a floor covering that can be taken up at a whim. Think of it as a marble floor, something that is yours forever.*")

A widow puts on her housedress and moves around the house, letting the dust gather on the end tables and the ledges of the windows. After the month she might go to lunch with some friends, but not to the movies where laughter sneaks up, and she forgets herself until she walks out into the afternoon light. Then it all floods back, the grieving.

Sooner or later, the widow loses the privilege of days of grieving. Or she might realize upon waking one morning that nothing is going to be the same again, at least not without some effort on her part. She has gotten used to the absence of effort and to other acts of repetition as useless as grieving, the mornings so motionless that she has to wonder what it was she did before. The food sits out too long on the counter. She had every intention of eating it until it was the moment for sitting down and picking up a fork or a spoon. No, absolutely, grieving is not something to be tolerated for too long, any more than wearing a veil serves any purpose but to hide from the necessities of getting on with it.

# Chapter Fourteen: Modesty

"Modesty," she tells the girls, "is essential to the concept of being a lady." She doesn't say that the role of a lady is an act that requires constant practicing, but it is also easy to discard. The throwing off is done in private without any traces so that there are only reports of it, which can be denied.

"So what is a lady?" she asks. "Let's think about."

"Manners."

"Wearing white gloves when you dress up."

"You can wear black gloves, too, but maybe only at night or in the winter."

"Having a nice house."

"Pretty clothes."

"Smiling all the time."

Kate won't say that a lady is a mannequin, naked in the windows of Hudson's at season change or before Easter. Sometimes her arms lie on the floor until they get the dress on her and pull her legs out of the sockets to put on the shoes. She isn't a lady until they get done with her, and she always has to go back to the plaster nakedness for maybe half a day until the window dresser arrives.

"Can you always be a lady?" And get what you want. She won't say that either. A mother will call the principal. "That woman said that every girl can be a whore if she wants to, and, of course, she wants to be a whore, everyone knows that. She just has to pretend to be a lady. The Family Living teacher, that's the one."

"Can you always be a lady?"

"If you watch yourself."

"Yes. And modesty is the first rule of protecting your role as a lady."

The illusion of modesty is better than the real thing.

# Chapter Fifteen: Housewarming

Kate loves her body, and she doesn't. But nakedness is what she has to offer when she meets a man. She wants her clothes to lie in little heaps on the floor, like in the movies; a stocking hanging over the arm of a chair, the shoe overturned near the door to the bedroom, slip crumpled up at the foot of the bed. She wants to be naked more than she wants to hide the faults of her body.

She has never told Michael about Casey; she isn't telling him that Casey taught her the ways of love. That Casey was always on to her.

"'Fee, fie, fo, fum. I smell the blood of an Englishman.' On you, Kate. You can't hide anything from the hunter."

Michael is her punishment for abandoning Casey when he was dying. She threw him off like an overcoat so that she could run naked through the riotous nights.

She can wait Michael out. For the time being, she is going to make another home. For Suliman-Gary-Al-Rashid-Johnson.

*"Girls, you wouldn't visit someone's house without bringing a house gift. That doesn't mean that you have to run to Target or Penney's, exceeding your gift budget. A little creativity is called for because the gift envelope is almost always empty. That's when the womanly arts come in handy. Write that down: womanly arts. Who knows what that means?"* The girls look down at their notebooks. *"The age-old arts. Of course, we don't weave any more, we don't need to, but there is still knitting and crocheting. Everyone has seen those darling pieces of needlework with cheerful messages, so carefully woven in and out of the backing. 'God Bless Our Happy Home.' 'A Smile is a Ray of Sunshine.' In the kitchen. That's where my mother kept my needlework.*

*"Baking. Chocolate chip cookies fresh in a tin box, you can get them at K-Mart. A basket with two wine glasses and a corkscrew, wrapped in a pretty napkin or even a dishcloth. When you are older, and there is a celebration—an engagement, the birth of a baby—use your imagination to come up with the right gift for the occasion."*

She is given out; there is nothing left, nothing that a man would want. But she will use her imagination.

It is after one o'clock when she parks her car on Aurelia. Two of the houses next to Suliman's house are empty, the windows broken. It is a bright winter afternoon, and the steep roofs of the houses are sharp against the sky; the walkways have been shoveled, and there are overturned pots on the porches, set aside for spring and summer flowers. Down the street the trees are old and thick; the houses won't be too hot in the summer.

When he opens the door, he is scowling. "Not that I ain't glad to see you, hungry as I am. But I thought, you being the considerate type, you would've been here earlier. The only things to eat around here are for the rats."

"At least you're glad to see me."

"Downstairs looks like a cave or a dungeon. Don't remember the paint peeling, and for sure I didn't leave a collection of old boxes when Reginald locked me out. That cat comes and goes in here like he pleases. Least he didn't touch my art. Then we have to be doing some talking.

"These ain't the living quarters. More like the workshop, nerve cell of the operation, know what I'm saying? Little desk used to be here for the interested customers and for putting down the brochures. Wonder what happened down here while I been gone. Second floor is still cool, nothing disturbed. Third floor is what I call home. You know, where I crash, got a little kitchen. Nothing in it, like I said."

"There's food. I didn't know what you liked, so I had to use my judgment."

"You went all out. Eggs, butter, sausage, lunchmeat, cheese. Plenty of stuff to fill my cupboard."

There are cans of paint and cartons on the floor, a box of tools, a crumpled scaffold.

"Don't look at this mess," he says, waving his hand over the brick floor and the patches of plaster on the walls that have not been painted over.

"Upstairs is a whole different story. Just let me have a little breakfast here, and you can have the grand tour. The art work of Suliman Al-Rashid, Esquire. I spent the whole night turning my stuff around, so they can see the sunlight again. Reginald, he turned them all to the wall. Guess they remind him of how he did me, locking me out. But, hey, I'm back, ain't I. Got my place back and a pretty little sponsor."

"Sponsor might not be the appropriate word today."

"Then how about my woman? Is that what you got in mind?"

"I haven't worked it out."

"Then let it happen. Whatever. I pay my debts. Well, so far you been doing the paying, but you'll get back everything you think is coming to you. Say the word. Like Suliman, you owe me."

"This is not the kind of conversation I like."

"We got to start with the truth, ain't that so? Hey, I don't mean to be getting at you. Let's fix us some food, break some bread together. Do our business later."

The stairs that lead to the second and third floors are splattered with paint.

"These are the slave quarters," Suliman says when they pass the second floor. "I mean to say that I'm the slave to my art. I don't mean racial stuff."

There is a kitchen on the third floor with a half refrigerator, a two-burner stove, a brown wooden table and two chairs. A pantry with open shelves and two cupboards. A closet of a bedroom.

"Bathroom's kinda dirty," he says, "but I gave it a few swipes, working with what I got. Which ain't a lot."

"I don't know where to start," Kate says.

"Look, you done your part. The rest is my problem."

She wants it to be her problem. Floors to scrub, sinks to scour, curtains to hang, walls to paint. A broom to wield. She will tie up her hair, and when he is pleased, he will untie the scarf. And then, and then.

"Are you saying that you don't need anything else?"

"Maybe you'll be the one saying you won't be needing anything else."

"Oh," she said, "I need."

"We can take care of that. All needs will be satisfied. You got my word."

Kate scrambles the eggs in a sauce pan and simmers the sausages in water in a battered pot before she grills them on the stove. There is no toaster, so she browns the bread in the oven. She makes instant coffee. There is no spatula, frying pan, or bread knife.

*"Tools—good, sturdy kitchen tools, girls—will last you a lifetime if you spend a few extra pennies. How many of you remember that special pan your mother used?"* No one raises her hand. *"I'll bet it was your grandmother's special pan as well, not something your mother got as a wedding gift. More chances than not, she and your father went out and bought the cheapest set of pots and pans that they could find, eight different sizes in a carton. That is a big mistake. So that special pan, maybe one of those cast iron frying pans that are practically antiques, that pan is responsible for some of your mother's best meals. Think about quality. Kitchen tools are as important to you as good tools are to a carpenter or an electrician.*

*"A quality chef's knife, a good toaster oven, a coffee pot with a metal carafe so that you aren't running out five minutes before company comes to replace the glass carafe that has just broken.*

*"I can't emphasize enough: good tools. Top of the line. But don't waste money where you don't have to. An inexpensive, basic microwave will do all you need because, face it, you aren't going to cook in your microwave. That's too iffy, and you will end up with a gray hunk of inedible meat and some mushy vegetables."*

"So how come it took you so long to get here? We're eating breakfast food and it's nearly time for supper."

"I had some difficulty leaving the house."

"Husband get in the way?"

"Who said I had a husband?"

"You don't need to say. I know the look of a woman who is in a bad mess of a marriage."

"It turned out that way."

"I can always tell."

*Michael was sitting in the kitchen reading the newspaper and drinking coffee. Mid-morning was his kitchen time in their silent arrangement. Two years ago? Three? How long had it been since they had spoken to each other?*

*"Michael." He didn't look up.*

*"Michael, say one word to me. That's all you have to do. Or everything will come tumbling down."*

*He left the table and went to the door that led to the garage. She heard the grinding of the garage door and the backward crunch of the tires on the ice.*

"*Your coat, Michael, you need your coat,*" *she called after him.*
"I was trying not to come here," she says.
"You made a big investment."
"I wasn't thinking of that."
"Then what?"
"I shouldn't be here. I don't want it, and you don't want it. We are standing at the entrance of hell."
"We ain't going to hell for eating some eggs now."
"I mean a personal hell."
"Well, that is strictly your choice. We can have a good time, or yeah, it can be hell, complaining and dissatisfaction. But I ain't got time for that. And you sure don't need it. No, that ain't a good idea, making something bad out of a basically good deal. You're helping me out, and I'm helping you out. Giving you a place to hang out. Ain't that what you want? Won't bother me. You're pretty nice for your age and all. Let's say we help each other out and leave hell to some other people. Me, I had enough of hell. No paints, no paper, nothing to draw, not even a little knife and a piece of wood to take up the time of day. If you ask me, that's what hell is, not having something to create, something to spin out of your head like a spider spins out his web."

Kate is crying.

"This isn't like me," she says.

"Maybe this is a different you, making room for another person in there."

She thinks she will never stop crying. Suliman waits, and then he raises her from the chair. "I'm holding on to you now, and you hold on to me. That way we're both going to be okay."

"I'll bet the sheets are dirty," she says.

"There ain't any sheets. Blanket neither. Hey, did that get your attention? Maybe I should be the one crying with no sheets and no blanket."

"That's terrible."

"I was happy. Least I had my things. And if I had a towel, I would say you should wash your face of all those tears. But there ain't any towels either."

"I have so many. I can...."

"You done enough."

"I want to come here. After school, on the weekends."

"Well, sure, but you need something to do. Like some interest to keep you busy because this ain't a love nest. It's an artist studio."

"I know you don't want to sleep with me."

"I'm not telling you lies. If you were in a line of women I'd be picking from, no, I wouldn't be choosing you. No insult, but there's a lot of young women out there, and it's only natural I take one of them. But, see, here you are, and I am getting used to you, you know what I'm saying. We could get it on, no trouble."

"That's no compliment."

"If all you need is a compliment, then these were pretty good eggs."

"I prefer being sought after."

"That guy at the party, did he do any seeking?"

"He isn't anything to me."

"But you two got together in spite of all that. Like I'm not passing judgment, but he's pretty young and not very courteous to a lady. Probably not the first time either. And you got to admit, he's a bit of a fag even though the two of you was talking and all."

"Don't let him hear that."

"That punk! It only needs one punch. But forget that. I set up the gallery, what with it being so cold in here all night. Come and take a look."

# Chapter Sixteen: Kingdoms Come

"So what do you think?"

Paintings line the walls of the second floor. Some are set up on easels; the three dimensional works are balanced on cubes and rectangles.

"All of these paintings are yours?"

"I'm having a big problem. Last night I was pretty excited, looking at my work. Then I see other people looking at them. 'What's in this guy's head,' they'd be saying. 'All these jungle animals and African landscapes.' I never saw any jungle animals, not even in a zoo. Put me in a boat and point me in the direction of Africa, the minute you turn your back, I'd be coming back to Detroit. And look here. JFK, Johnson, Luther King, all these children playing under the flag. They don't mean nothing to me. Just paint on cardboard. Some broken glass and wire stuck in the picture, stuff I thought was cool.

"Man, I remember being so excited painting my first African mask. I wanted to yell, look at the African American artist, doing a real African mask. Only it ain't African and it ain't real.

"I need to find something real for me."

He is lost in the speculation of his paintings.

She is waiting for the moment that she can touch him in a way that he will know what the next step is. Then he will turn to her, circle her wrist with his hand as if he were giving her a bracelet. Or he will grasp her shoulders and lean to kiss her. She shudders. The kiss, it is always surprising, and then it is too late to go back. The kiss is the contract. It tells you everything.

But the revelation of Suliman's kiss is something she is afraid of. What if there is no connection? She needs a place to go every day until it is midnight; when Michael is in the house, and it is safe to go home. The two of them, under the same roof, slipping into sleep where they can still belong to each other.

"Now look at this," Suliman says. "This is one big disappointment. All those days, laying around that motel, thinking about my last project, and the limelight going right past me, and lighting on someone else when it's supposed to be me.

"Yeah, just laying in the bed, thinking about 'Kingdoms Come.' Not about dying. Don't get me wrong. That's what I call this project. I call it a project because I can't call it a canvas. Canvas strictly for the white man. Not that I'm bitter. In fact, the white man did me a favor, putting canvas out of my reach. He gave me the leftovers, you know what I'm saying? Cardboard, old wood, cheap paper I got to size and prime until it can take the weight of paint. He leaves me charcoal, some old pencils, chalk. He puts the oils up high on the shelf so someone like me won't slip a few of them into my pocket or maybe in my hat. Plunk it back on my head, full of those little tubes of gold. Might as well be gold. Black man is thinking to himself, hey

I'm going to be an artist, too. White man says, here, boy, you can have the house paint, whatever is left over, so what if the color's all wrong. Or, look what we invented for you, acrylic paint, cheap and shiny. Like giving beads to the Indians.

"You ask me, the Indians are more stupid than Nee-groes because they started out with something and ended up with zip, zero, nada."

Suliman is a volcano.

Kate doesn't like the word, Negro, the way he snarls it. All the hatred bursts into the room like a bomb.

"Man, I don't even know what to think about 'Kingdoms Come.'"

The surface is crowded, a dark, layered background of purple and green. Buildings, skyscrapers and tenements form the horizon above the figure of an Egyptian goddess. Suliman points to the goddess. "This here is Isis, big-time figure in the African world. And these are her guard dogs," he says about two fierce lions looking outward at two fearful worshipers kneeling before the altar.

"Here we got two angels, Christian ones, but underdeveloped, with little stumps of wings, not the big feathery kind. You get the meaning. Maybe it's too political, but, hey, the artist's vision got a mind of its own. Isis, she's the important one here, but see, she's got some double natures in her. On her crown is the Star of David."

Isis stands in profile, her body ample and decorated with the shapes and colors of jewels. Her headdress resembles a boat that might have floated down the Nile. The goddess is facing an elaborate border of small figures that runs vertically down the painting. Two six-pointed stars separate Isis from the lines of brown and black faces, the figures dressed in white.

"But actually, she ain't the point. She's the beginning and the end. These here are the guys that really count." Suliman points to the figure of a man at the edge of the painting as if he were entering its world. "Leonardo, that artist could do anything he set his mind to. And Gabriel here, he's the archangel. Only this Gabriel, he's a black angel."

Gabriel is a large, dark shadow, an angel in a storm cloud.

"Isn't he the angel of death?"

"That's the whole point, he's the really powerful one, dark as death. Ain't that the way it's going? The black man is the death of white people. Not to mug you on the street but to slip into your whiteness and make it dark. Make us all one.

"So I show Gabriel blowing the trumpet, announcing the fact that kingdoms are coming, coming together, gathering at the feet of this little lamb, but they're bigger than the lamb. They're going to overwhelm this little white lamb with the weight of history.

"Suliman, my name, means peace, but when I'm painting, I don't feel peaceful. I feel angry when I'm caught up in the work. Man, it is my life. Only maybe you don't like my art. It never occurred to me to ask you what kind of art you like."

"I don't have any preferences about art."

"So, okay, what you think of this stuff?"

"It seems busy."

"Too much going on. I can see that myself. And you don't have to say you like my work. Because you know what, something is seriously wrong here."

"It's not wrong. You're a good artist. But I don't know. I don't have any experience with art."

"Come on now, they drag every kid in the world kicking and screaming to the art museum. Me, I was pretending not to look, but I went back on my own. Took the bus to look at some pictures of people in weird clothes, looking out of the canvas like a photographer was at the other end. I mean, looking real. So I start sketching what was real, come to find out real ain't what it's all about. Every time I turn around, art is about something else. Right now, standing here, you looking with your eyes, I'm seeing what you're seeing. A bunch of junk."

"Suliman, you didn't get much sleep, and so much has been happening...."

"Ain't nothing happening but me finding out that I ain't the artist I thought I was. Should've stayed a kept man in the Fairlane. That's what I think after looking at this stuff.

"See here. Color like mud, and a bird looking like a turkey when I was painting a dove. I had me a good time, slapping on the paint like it was water. Texturing my dove, I told myself. Making a symbol of peace. That is a lie because the last thing I am all about is peace, no matter what name they gave me."

"Maybe you should consider what you would really like to do. With your art."

"You ain't my teacher, know what I'm saying? You ain't in a position to be the judge of me."

"I'm just trying...."

"You just waiting to get what you came for."

"No, I...."

"Well, Miss Kate, I can't do it. No offense, but I do not feel like performing. I just got the shock of my life, and it affects my nature. My manly nature. In fact, if you want to know the truth, I want to cry."

Kate doesn't look at Suliman. She looks instead at an orange and yellow sky like a blaze of fire. The Lincoln Memorial is burning, the small flames eating up the walls. She could be wrong; it might be a temple. She is afraid to ask. People are watching, dark against the burning sky: a man holding a baby away from the flames; four other figures, also dark, closer to the flames, more interested, she thinks, than afraid.

"This is good," she says. "It's telling a story.

"It ain't nothing. But this ain't bad. Look here. Maybe I can find a little redemption. I call this one 'Generations of Angels.'"

The angels, black women in flowing dresses with wide sleeves, are lifting their arms in gestures of joy. They are welcoming an infant in swaddling clothes and a halo that looks like the sun. At their feet, there are creatures that look like snails and peacocks. They might be plants.

"Even though I am not a Christian any more, I have respect for the symbols. My Muslim brothers have some problems with this, but I spent my youth"—he says "youf"—"in church. Well, let's say I had to go, part of the program.

"We get in the van, hair all patted down, wearing the clean shirt they give us, checking to see if our trousers is creased up good. We go to the only church letting in the boys from Juvey. Juvenile delinquents sitting in the back of the van, going to the Baptist Church. No one asks if someone might be a Catholic or a Methodist or whatever. And there's a lot more of the same to be telling if you aren't walking out of the door any time soon."

"Do you want me to leave? I feel like I am being pushed out of the door, not walking out."

"Yes and no. Like I am a man in crisis, about my art, you know. Look how I let Linda make me her personal slave! All I needed was a fan to keep her cool while she's sleeping like Cleopatra. I was stuck in a bad place. Sure, I could've found a job, maybe stay with relatives, but I gave up. Linda comes along. Far as she's concerned, having money is being sexy, and making it in bed is the same as love. Bad choice for a bad time.

"I know love and I know sex. Nine times out of ten, love holds more together than sex. Twenty minutes later, you forget about sex. Love you got forever even when the person isn't around. Know what I'm saying? That dude you were toting around? I didn't see any love. Him using you, you using him. So who do you love? Your old man, I mean your husband?"

"My husband, Michael, broke our contract," she says. "And I don't have to apologize about Stephon or about you."

"Well, so far I ain't the issue. We haven't got there yet. How come you and Michael don't split. Like go to divorce court."

"It isn't that simple."

"You got property?"

"The house. And the mortgage."

"Guess neither of you have anything if you don't sit around in the same house hating each other."

"It isn't about hate."

"It sure ain't about love."

But it is about love, the absence of love, the shadow figure of Michael more substantial than the men with black skin over muscle, brown skin against her paleness. He is the image; the men who have replaced him, Stephon, LaMar, Curtis, are the negatives, the dark part of love. Michael is the husband, permanent, white, powerful.

"Leaving isn't possible," she says.

"That is some weird arrangement. Far as I can see, the two of you are making life real hard. But if you need a place to stay, you got it. You're paying the rent. You don't have to stay in the house with a dude who's not doing his duty. In fact, ain't that the plan?"

"I like going home. I like knowing it's there. My daughter....."

"Don't tell me she's living in this bad dream, too?"

"No, but she would want us to be together."

"I sure ain't buying that. Well, you work it out. But look here, I want to show you some more stuff. This problem with my art is getting to me big time.

"Something is wrong, a big mistake. I can hear the white dudes laughing. 'Black man thinks he can pay a tribute to Picasso by painting some screaming horse.' That's what this is, would you believe it? Some people looking at this might not think I even heard of Picasso."

The canvas is large and the color of flames; the horse rears up, his upper body arching toward the cooling blue, sucked back by the orange burst of color. The eyes roll back, the teeth show.

"I like it."

"You said yourself you don't got art experience."

"I can like something. And not like something."

"There's plenty here not to like. Look here."

Small black figures cower before a panther about to leap out of a triangle of light. In the distance there's the Capital Building and the figure of Abraham Lincoln. In the foreground is a white figure bent over a bowl. Doves fly over the black figures. Suliman shakes his head.

"I can't even remember what I call this. Stupid, probably. I've been fooling myself, calling myself an artist. So you regretting this now?"

"It's not the artist part that bothers me."

"Yeah, but that's part of the package. Else it's another motel room, another schedule."

"It's the house, this house. It isn't the right place."

"All my stuff is here. Paintings half started, everything in the right place except where that Reginald moved stuff around."

"You need a fresh start."

"Like I got any money. Besides, you gave him advance rent."

"It was just for a month. To give us time to look around."

"Like a halfway house, you mean."

"Something like that."

"Reginald will pitch a fit about turning up the heat."

"Reginald isn't going to know anything until he comes around for the next month's rent."

"Tell you the truth, Miss Kate, there ain't much in it for you."

"It's something to look forward to."

"Folks need something of their own to look forward to. Some kind of passion. I don't mean painting or stuff like that. Maybe you like to write some poems. Or knit. Maybe even embroider. Lots of women like to embroider, make up their own stories with a needle.

"Yeah, when I think of a woman making art, I can just see her, really see her, weaving or leaning over a piece of cloth, telling a story with needles."

"I don't have any particular talents."

"Everyone has a talent. You need to investigate. Do you like cooking? Decorating? Stuff like that, it all comes out to be talent. Maybe you never dreamed up your talent yet. Like me when I was at Ellis Island—it was sort of like a prison, depending how you look at it. Yeah, I spent eight months in a criminal's paradise until I got stupid and broke the rules. But while I was there, one of my jobs was carving, simple stuff on wood, like designs on drawers and the backs of mirrors.

"I said to the supervisor, 'You wasting good wood,' but he gave me a design to follow, and I took off like a bird.

"I didn't know it was in me to carve. I still remember how it felt, my hand around that chisel, making the first cut, the wood giving way to the pressure of my hand, life springing up out of the wood. You know what it felt like? Baptism. When folks come up out of the water after getting dunked, they got a new light in their eyes. Maybe it is only from being glad not to drown, the preacher forgetting to let them up in time while he is talking about Jesus and sins getting washed away.

"When I am doing anything, carving, painting, working with clay or just sanding something down, I feel baptized. I feel new. So you got to find something that makes you feel baptized into newness."

"It's love. Making love."

"Man, that's like eating. Life's big necessity. If I had to choose between art and sex, sex is the loser. Even if I don't like what I'm seeing here today, I guess I'm committed to it until I find the real thing, the true vision God meant me to have. When that comes, I wouldn't have time to be thinking about sex."

"That's all I'm good at."

"Can't believe that, Miss Kate."

"Why are you calling me that?"

"Because I owe you so much. And I want to respect my betters."

Kate laughs. "I am not your better. I am just the woman with money borrowed from the Detroit Teachers Credit Union. And my Christmas envelope. Money doesn't make a person better. It makes them the one doing the giving."

"Well, I owe you, and I am going to pay you back. The only thing you like. That's the payment."

"You do not want to have sex with me."

"Hey, I'm a man, ain't I?"

"You would be pretending. I like the real thing. It has a life of its own, good sex. Otherwise, it is like eating breakfast or taking a shower."

"It would make me happy to love you. No kidding. But you're right. I don't have the feeling. Some place we missed the Pretend Bus that could have taken us to bed."

"We'll have to find another bus."

# Chapter Seventeen: Works in Progress

Kate goes to the art museum. She likes the sculpture and the perfection of the male body.

Suliman is as beautiful as a statue, muscular and delineated as if he had been made of stone; her stone lover with a "Do Not Touch" sign on the pedestal where she has placed him.

In the car—she lets him drive even though he does not have a license—she touches the flat plane of his cheek. He doesn't turn his head away from her. The way that Michael would. And Casey when he was angry. He only did that once. She can swear to that. But she was desirable then.

Sleeping with him or never sleeping with him, there is no way to talk about it; there is only the careful way they are with each other in the car, in the house that they are packing up, in the art stores, in Target and Home Depot.

She doesn't like to buy his clothes at Target. Saks or Neiman-Marcus would be more like it. She would buy him a leather jacket, fine woolen slacks, alpaca sweaters, and shirts that cost over $100 and have to be ironed.

His lovely foot, the long bones, would be shod in Italian leather. "Shod," that's a word she pulls up from a schoolgirl memory and a teacher speaking:

"*It means to be shoed. Now we only think of horses being shod. But it's a beautiful word that belongs to the elegant, sculpted foot.*"

Suliman's foot is elegant. His naked foot, unshod. When she comes in, he is painting or arranging his supplies, barefoot on the cement floor of the first floor studio. He is quick to cover his feet.

"Time got away from me. I got to get decent now that a lady is here."

"It's okay. I've seen feet before."

"My mama said that bare feet belong to pickaninnies and whores."

He pulls on his white socks and searches around for his battered gym shoes. It's too cold to be barefoot in this house where the furnace beats out heat in bursts and heaves, but that's the way he likes to paint.

"It's a habit I got into way back."

She doesn't ask him about the times before. He will tell her when he wants to.

They have been looking for a new studio. One floor with partitions to divide the workspace from the gallery space and good ventilation because of paint fumes. Suliman says that he can build anything if he has a tool and some wood.

"Place where I was, Ellis Island, we learnt how to do just about anything with wood. I got designs right in my head for whatever is going to be needed."

The kitchen will be a problem if there isn't a stove. She has already been to ABC Warehouse, pricing the refrigerators and the stoves. The new studio will be her place, too.

He is finishing up the last piece, the one he had begun when it was the end of the month, and there was no money for the next month, no way to talk Reginald into another week.

The colors are dark: blue, brown, and black. Three small boys are looking over the shoulder of the protector, a big boy, wearing a drooping white undershirt. The smaller boys are wearing shirts with collars, buttoned to the neck.

"These little kids are the innocent ones who need protection. But the protector has to know what's going on. Or he can't do his job, keeping evil away from the children."

In the background are sketches of the White House and an eagle hovering over it. Suliman taps the sketches with a brush. "Evil always got a shape. It ain't a cloud, and it ain't a red devil with a pitchfork. No, evil is something we see every day. Sometimes we don't even know it's evil. Like these kids, fresh out of their mamas' arms and into the street. No one to protect them but him. From this." He taps the eagle again.

He wants to finish this painting, because he says that it's the last of a series and something new is coming, something big and different.

"Like I never been an artist before I started having this vision. Only it ain't complete. The vision is coming, but it ain't here."

Kate never corrects him. When he speaks correctly, he is angry or hurt. She likes the way the words come out slipping and sliding and arranging themselves in patterns that are his own creations.

"Danger, that's the theme of this painting. Art got a job, teach kids how to survive. Only these paintings, they are not doing the job. But you can't rush into the river, know what I mean? It flows on by until it's your turn to step into it. But I am sure impatient. To find the next thing, to know how to be."

Kate sees a holy light in Suliman. She wants to be the keeper of the light.

But she does not know the difference between heat and light.

# Chapter Eighteen: The New Place

"The new studio needs lots of light. All my life I been dreaming about having a skylight," Suliman says. "I ain't saying to turn the city upside down for a skylight. Probably cost too much. The place can't be the whole thing. You seen how much supplies cost.

"You ought to cut me loose, Kate. Every day is a taking day, me taking from you. Like the other people, she took it out of my skin. I am telling you, she drained me dry, getting her money's worth."

"I'm getting my money's worth."

"I don't see myself doing any giving. Makes me ashamed. Like I don't have any upbringing." He laughs. "Don't know why I say that because I don't have any upbringing to speak of. But I do have sense about how things should be with people. Well, you'll get your due. Wait and see."

Kate has done her taking. It is time for paying back, not in tens and twenties but in terms of devotion. Devotion is what she feels for Suliman. She won't call it love. She has used up love: with Casey, with Michael, with Shannon.

*"Girls, it is important for the entire family that you take time out for yourself. After all, you will be the homemaker, the mother, and the nurturer. Everything is your responsibility, starting with those little sacks of lunch you will prepare each night to the last dish that has to be taken from the drain board and put back in its place. Everything has to be in its place if home is to be the safe haven and the refuge it is meant to be." The girls look up at the references to safe haven, refuge. Is she talking about war or a shelter for abused women? They never ask. The words are written in their notebooks and then forgotten as if she never said them. "The nurturer, it is a form of the word, nutrition." She writes both words on the board. "Everything needs nutrition. And people need nurturing. Sometimes both nurturing and nutrition can be the same thing. It could be something simple like a glass of milk and a soft-boiled egg. Or a favorite meal. It can be ironing your daughter's dress while she is sleeping to wear in the morning, fresh and starched and hanging on her coat tree, the one you painted with flowers and raindrops. That's just an example," she says, putting up her hand to stop them from writing down "coat tree," "painted flowers," and "raindrops."*

*"All that nurture must come from somewhere, right? It is coming from you, and from time to time, you have to lay in a fresh supply. You have to replace it. Does anyone know how you replace something that is inside of you that can't be seen?"*

*"Going shopping."*

*"Getting a massage."*

*"Praying for guidance."*

*"Good answers, all good answers. You have to do something for yourself. It isn't all sacrifice, but it isn't all reward, tit for tat"—they laugh, it is an old phrase, probably with meanings she didn't intend. "Nurturing yourself can be an early*

*morning walk after the kids have gone to school. Or reading a book while the baby is napping. Candlelight at dinner when your children are at their grandparents. That special time that only two people can share, married people."*

They had written these platitudes in their notebooks. Then they must have thrown them away because there were plenty of cast-off notebooks lying on the floor when school let out for the summer. No one ever came back to tell her that she had shown them the right way to live.

No, it wasn't the right way. It was just the way she thought that women should be: giving and giving until they were wrung dry.

She is parched. She is dying of thirst. She wants to stop at a 7-Eleven and get a Coke. But they are on the Davison Freeway, and the small stores that used to be part of an old avenue have been boarded up or torn down.

They are looking for a street in Hamtramck that runs off Joseph Compeau, Evaline.

"Guy who told me about this place says I'm gonna like it," he says. "Quiet street with store buildings on the corners." Suliman moves his finger on the map tracing his way to the street.

"'Course, Hamtramck ain't my favorite place. I always stay on the West Side. Seems like they got more trees on the West Side. Or something. Over here seems like a colder place even though on the weather the temperature's always a little higher on the East Side. Like it ain't even in the same Detroit. But this guy says this is the place that's been waiting for me."

"Who is this 'guy'?"

"Just a guy I know. Met him the other night. Came by after you left. We got to talking, boom, he has just the place for me. It sounds just right. Even though it's in Hamtramck."

"Is he the owner?"

"No, he's hooking me up with the place. Hey, you got to turn right here."

"Is he Polish? Hamtramck is a Polish neighborhood."

"Well, this brother ain't Polish."

She is paying the rent and buying the food and providing the materials. Suliman should be in the house, day and night, giving Kate her money's worth. He should be finishing the painting, getting ready for the next project. Or he should be labeling the cartons with the names of the contents: acrylics, watercolors, paint thinners, brushes, chalks, pencils, and charcoals. He should be building frames for stretching canvas over the wood she has bought at a lumberyard that was going out of business.

"How did he know where to find you?"

"Here it comes, the interrogation. 'Where have you been?' 'How do you know him?' 'Why don't you stay in the house twenty-four-seven like a good boy?' Okay, I'm going to tell you. I met him at the bar on Trumbull couple nights ago. That's right. I spent some of those precious dollars that you dole out of your little change purse like you giving charity. For my emergency needs. Like you're the Red Cross. But I didn't buy iodine or Band-Aids or aspirin. I bought a beer. That was my emergency. And then this guy, he buys me a beer. And I buy him a beer. With the dimes and the quarters I get for allowance. Just an exaggeration, right? Because you're about to say that you give me plenty of walking around money. That you don't carry a little change purse. But that's what it feels like. Like you are my granny giving me candy money from your little purse, and it is killing you, every penny you give me.

"Maybe it's not a good idea, going to look at this new place. Because we have developed a communication problem and a generation gap problem. And that's two problems too many."

"Suliman, I am sorry. Please. Close the car door. We need to see this place. I couldn't imagine.... We can't spoil the plans.... I am sorry."

"We're just gonna look at the place. No negotiations. The future is something we don't know about right now."

Kate is afraid that she will faint because she can't endure what she is afraid to lose. When she recovers, the whole world will be different like the first time.

*Standing in the kitchen in her slip, she swallows the antihistamine that has been in the medicine cabinet, she doesn't know how long. She feels a cold coming on, but she wants to go out. Then she is sinking down, not unconscious, but not seeing. She hears the whir of the refrigerator and the clicking of the water heater as if they were sounds of waterfall and earthquake. Michael comes into the kitchen; she can hear the tap-tap of his footsteps. She says his name, but it is the dry whisper of wind that begins in her throat and never becomes a sound. She cannot see him, but she feels him there. Then there are the sounds of walking, tap-tap, tap-tap. And the side door slamming shut.*

*No, she can't faint again. She needs all of her senses to keep it together. Everything can be buried. Michael walking away. Shannon talking to someone on the phone. Shouting at her father, "Why did you leave her?"*

*Suliman, who owes her everything, waits until she goes home and slips out of the side door.*

"I don't want you to leave, Suliman."

"Can't see why you want me to stay."

Yes, you do. Yes, you do.

The new studio is perfect. That's what Suliman says, but to Kate, it is just a blank space, four white walls, enormous.

"Man, it is my dream come true. I can see it now. Movable walls. We get right to work and make some partitions out of plywood. Put little casters on them, wheels too unstable. We have a show, move them out. We need a little privacy, we make some little rooms. They can be different sizes, different colors. Maybe two or three colors, but nothing too tacky."

"There's no stove."

"I can use a hot plate. You know, Ramen noodles, Cup-a-Soup."

"Maybe at Salvation Army, I can get a...."

"You're in charge of decorating, Kate. Ain't that what you do anyway?"

"I teach Family Living, sometimes clothing. Not foods any more. It got too expensive."

"There you go then. This place is right up your alley."

Shannon will never come home again. Kate can paint her bedroom set. Michael won't ask, but if he did, she would say that she sold it, and people are coming to get it. But not the mattress. Suliman can't sleep on her daughter's mattress even if it means spending more money as if her pockets are deep. Every day she reaches into her pockets for Suliman, hoping they won't be empty.

She'll have to teach summer school. The new studio will cost so much money. The stove, a refrigerator. New bathroom fixtures, faucets, and the toilet seat is so filthy. Home Depot. But Shannon's bedroom set is a start. The mattress can be ordered and delivered right away. He needs to sleep and he needs to eat.

He needs her. She cannot tolerate the losses if he doesn't need her.

The rent is $600 a month for bare walls and a cement floor that holds the cold. She will have to find floor tiles, affordable ones, but that's okay. She has done it before, tiled a floor. She has plastered, painted, repaired.

*"If you can read, girls, then you can take care of those small but expensive breakdowns. You might not be able to afford a plumber or a washing machine repairman. There are going to be some things that you simply can't afford. But you will be able to manage the cost of a book or a do-it-yourself manual. The government has books—and they are free—about how to make repairs. There are household magazines. You will need a few tools, not too cheap, because you don't want to replace them. If you are prepared to make your own repairs, your household budget won't get out of control.*

*"Your toilet, for example, is a basic construction. Has anyone here ever lifted the lid on the toilet tank?"* No one raises her hand. *"Well, what do you think is in there?"*

"Water."

"A rubber ball."

*"A process is set in motion when you flush the toilet. You just don't pull on the handle and presto, it's flushed. No, the handle releases a trap in the tank. The water flows down and the bulb sinks to the bottom of the tank. Then the water begins to rise. We can hear it stop, and when it doesn't, we know something has gone wrong. Then what would you do?"*

"Tell my dad."

"Call my mother."

"Say it was my brother's fault."

*"You repair that toilet yourself, armed with the government booklet and replacement parts from the hardware store. Don't worry about mistakes. Making mistakes means that you are learning."*

There is only a sink and a toilet.

"You got second thoughts, Kate, about being the woman behind the man?"

"I'm thinking about this place."

"I hope you having positive thoughts. Because I'm having some positive thoughts. You going all the way with me, no ifs, ands, or buts. Tell you the truth, I like the way you are. Oh, you're too old for me, we both know that, but when you start thinking about making things happen, a light come on, and, girl, you are beautiful. And about twelve years old. Anyway, that's what I'm seeing."

"I'll try to keep the light on," she says.

"Don't be bothered because I'm gonna be remembering it from now on."

He turns toward her. "You did it for me. Made all my dreams real. Don't ever think I'm gonna forget it. You're gonna be the queen of all of this."

He will crush her, but not with his weight. She wants his weight. She wants to be with him in his dream. But he will crush her with his exuberance. He will crush her as if she were an old piece of lace, no use to him, not even to clean a brush with or wipe across a canvas.

"You're feeling the happiness, too. Right? About the studio. All the things that are happening."

"Of course. Yes."

"So why don't we get happy together"

Kate knows this: Their lovemaking is a reflection of some other passion. Suliman is celebrating his happiness. But he isn't with her; he is inside of his joy. She doesn't complain.

# Chapter Nineteen: Moving Men

Men in rattling trucks come to the house to move the paintings, the easels, the boxes of paints, thinners, brushes; the containers of rags, beads, stones, rope and yarn; the stretchers, the burlap, the scanty roll of linen canvas. How does Suliman know them? How do they know to come to the house at this specific time? There is no phone in the Aurelia house.

The men don't call Suliman by his name. They call him "man" or "bro." When the trucks are loaded, they wait for Suliman to lock up the house and walk over to where Reginald is standing on his porch.

"This all the notice you giving me, man? After what I done for you."

"You didn't give me no notice the day you put me out."

"No rent for three months, that's plenty of noticing to me. You didn't notice that no money changed hands?"

"We're gonna put all this behind us, Reginald. We're gonna part like gentlemen. You been square with me. You could have thrown my stuff out in the street. But you been fair. Me, I've been as fair as I can afford. Can't be asking my lady to go the poorhouse over me. You know what I mean, man. Can't be asking for the impossible."

"What you got to say to that, Miss Kate? This guy bleeding you white?"

Reginald wants her to pay and to pay more than she can afford to even the score, the score that is always being kept.

"That would be accurate, Mr. Calvert."

"I didn't even take no deposit to be holding back."

"There just ain't no more money, Reginald. You want a painting, fine. Take your pick. But we are plain out of coins."

"Now what would I want with a painting, Suliman? They ain't nothing to me. I ain't no African. I don't care nothing about eagles and leopards in the jungle. Or little black kids picking cotton. That ain't my reality. This is my reality. My real estate. A couple houses in a neighborhood that The Man don't want no more. They come to me by default, you know what I'm saying. And the property that I got, even though they only the leftovers, that is what I am interested in.

"Fine, you got empty pockets right now. If you ask me, without Miss Kate here and her pretty little checks, your pockets always gonna be empty if all you got to paint is something that probably don't even exist any more. The jungle. Animals. What do that mean to me?"

"No need to run me down, man. Not over a few dollars. We don't got it to give and saying hurtful stuff not going to change it."

"Truth sometimes be hurtful."

"I ain't taking you serious, Reginald, because all you want is more money. And a man who only live for money, he just ain't in the position to know about an artist. One day you be coming by and saying to me, 'Hey, Suliman, remember when you say I could have a painting? I come for it.' I'll give it to you, man, but it's gonna be worth more than you deserve. It's gonna be a painting by Suliman Al-Rashid, and it will be talking to you."

# Chapter Twenty: Detective Work

The new space is painted white. The small windows do not admit enough light. Suliman wants to break them out and build new window frames. Kate asks him what he knows about tearing down and building. He says he knows how to do things because he wasn't given a choice. But not having a choice was a gift, too, because from the time he learned to hold a hammer correctly and to join edges together, he has not stopped creating things.

"When we ain't so busy, getting set up, you know, then I'll tell you my life story, backwards and forwards. And then maybe you tell me a little bit about yourself."

They are too busy. After school Kate goes to Home Depot and Lowe's. She wants paste-on tiles for the floor, but with cushion and substance. They are expensive, eighty-nine cents a tile, and there are so many to buy. The clerk tells her to go to the tile outlet in Wixom where she can get seconds. "Nothing wrong with them. Tiny flaws, but we can't sell 'em."

Wixom after school and there is a freezing rain, but eighty-nine cents times 200 is too costly.

The tile outlet is behind a row of industrial shops, and it takes two trips up and down Wixom Road to find it. Fifty-six cents a tile. She can't multiply fast enough. "Hundred twenty one, counting tax," the woman says, "but you got to load them yourself." Kate says she'll come back for the tiles. "Can't guarantee that these exact tiles will still be here. Best to take them now."

She is fifty-eight years old, and she is loading tiles, ten to a pack, in the trunk of her car and on the back seat. The woman is reading a magazine. She looks up. "Sorry we don't have take-out service."

It is after seven in the evening when she gets to the studio with the tiles.

"The tiles cost one hundred and twenty-one dollars," she says to Suliman, who is lying on a pallet supported by two ladders and painting the ceiling.

"Glad to see you're in a good mood."

"I'm soaking wet."

"Did you bring any food?"

"I have a car full of tiles."

"There's room for some burgers."

"It's cheaper to make the food myself."

"The stove ain't connected. Can't call the gas company without a telephone."

"I'll go out for sandwiches."

"You know where to find me."

The telephone has been an ongoing argument.

"Who am I going to call?"

"Then why do you want it?"

"A man has business to do. This is the modern age, and I can't go writing letters."

"I'll get you a cell phone."

"Better than nothing, but it sure don't make the gallery official. No regular phone number. Just a pay-as-you-go cell phone."

Suliman has dreams, but she can't talk to him about them. There is the morning, and she wouldn't want to ruin that, and when she comes from school, there is too much to do. Then she is too tired to argue.

Every day there is another expense. There is no end to it, and the studio isn't finished. The stove—it's a two-burner—has to be hooked up, and that means calling the gas company. The refrigerator is second-hand, but she had to pay cash for it and give twenty dollars each to the two silent men who appeared out of nowhere to move it to the studio. Suliman never says who they are or how he knows them.

The detective of Kate's imagining is relieved when she leaves the studio at midnight. Then he can go off-duty. He doesn't have to follow her home after the first few times. He can go straight to the studio in the mornings instead of following her at 5:30. That's the time she leaves the house in jeans and a sweatshirt, carrying the tote bag with the clothes for school and her makeup. The detective might wonder why she doesn't start leaving things at the studio, but then he would reason that she didn't want to leave any evidence.

The detective is not hired to know about Suliman except that he exists, so he does not hear Suliman's complaints every time she leaves a pair of jeans or a sweater. "This is an artist studio, not no home." The detective does not know that Suliman keeps Kate's toothbrush under the sink or that her shoes, the ones she wears when they are painting, are stored at the back of the closet.

The detective doesn't hear Kate ask, "Why do you hide my things?"

"Don't like nothing out of place."

The paints, the acrylics, the brushes, the rolls of paper are lined neatly on shelves that have been hung from metal strips drilled into the wall. The shelves themselves have been painted white. The detective will not know that Suliman wants everything to be white, although he will probably notice—when the doors open and close—that there is no color in the studio.

Perhaps the detective has stood under a window and heard Suliman talk about color.

"If I knew the color of the universe, the color of the beginning, then it would be the color of these walls, this floor, this ceiling. Everything would be the color that comes from God. But I don't know. No place in the Bible is there any talk of the first color of things. First, I thought it had to be blue, but once I saw how many shades of blue I could come up with by myself, I got all weighed down with the blue idea. White is just my substitute until I get the final knowledge."

Suliman's art is determined by his visions, but that is not the detective's business. He is not a detective assigned to report conversations; he is a detective of events. If Kate came face to face to the detective and said, "I know you are following me," he wouldn't say anything to her. He would be like Michael.

Suliman has taken out the windows and widened the space. He has made new window frames, placing the panes of glass in the grooves that are precisely edged. He wants to paint the window frames white, but Kate says that the natural wood will make the windows look like paintings.

He is waiting for the big vision. "Can't do anything until I know exactly what is meant for me to paint." Kate doesn't ask questions about his painting. Her questions are about who and where and when.

She is at the studio as much as is possible. The detective will report that to Michael. He will also record that she is scrupulous about arriving at school on time and not leaving until after the 3:10 bell rings. She won't bring attention to herself by altering the schedule she has followed for years. She could carry her coat during hall duty and be ready to leave a little early, but she isn't doing that.

Kate gets up at five in the morning and at 5:30 she drives from Southfield to Hamtramck, fourteen miles away. People are out on the road, but traffic isn't as bad as it is at 7:10, which is the latest possible time she can leave the studio to get to the west side high school where she teaches. If she leaves Suliman's studio at 7:15, then she will be late for school because of the heavy traffic.

She is breathless when she reaches for the key to the studio, which is separate from her other keys. If she should leave it on the kitchen counter with her other keys, Michael would know about the studio and about Suliman. She can't take a chance about the key's power to expose her.

The key is attached to a silver shamrock. It has nothing to do with Suliman and cannot hint of his existence. She is careful about hiding every clue, although it is laughable even to her. She is a woman who leaves the house at five in the morning and doesn't return until midnight.

Suliman will reach for her in his sleep and make love to her before he is fully awake. She doesn't want him to be fully awake. She wants to be with him in his dream, and she is part of it, the dream of every morning.

When she opens the door, she rubs the shamrock for good luck. Let him be there. Let him be sleeping, and I will kiss his eyes, I will kiss his mouth.

There is so little time; there is only time to slip into his dream.

"Breakfast time," she says, and he moves toward her.

She never has breakfast, and there is no time to finish drinking her coffee when she gets to school. She is breathless, hungry, and disheveled.

The typing teacher asks her if she has a fever. "Yes," she says, "I am burning up."

Her students must notice that she is not as carefully made-up as she has been in the past, the eyes outlined precisely with a black pencil and her lashes brushed with brown-black mascara. Now her lashes are fading to colorlessness. "Miss Connally letting herself go, you noticing that?"

The teachers do notice, and they say, "Girl, you look a wreck. Got you a new man? I know you not seeing that sneaky Stephon any more because he got himself a woman who comes up to the school, making sure he's where he says he is."

"Serves him right," says Kate, but she doesn't say anything about Suliman.

The detective has to wait until she goes back to her classroom, unlocks the closet, puts on her coat and changes her shoes, and then walks to the parking lot. He will start his engine at 3:17 because she reaches the parking lot at 3:18.

If there is an accident on the Davison Freeway or a traffic problem on I-75 southbound, it will take both of them, Kate and the detective, more than half an hour to get from the school parking lot to the studio. Longer in rain or snow. They might have to take the service drive with all its twists and turns in order to reach Caniff Street, crowded with all the stores that are opening again, the boutiques and studios and cafes. It is the renovation of Hamtramck. The detective will notice the changes if he has been at his work for a long time.

There are no clues to inform Kate or the detective if Suliman is in the studio, or if he has gone off on his missions. There is no car or absence of a car to serve as a signal. No lights are turned on. "That's why the windows got to be so big," Suliman has said. "I rely on natural light."

She is always afraid she has forgotten the key, or that it has somehow fallen from her purse during the day. Perhaps the detective has his own key. When Kate has left for the night, he could look in at Suliman sleeping. Perhaps he stays behind at night and watches Suliman slipping into the other life he is leading in her absence. Then he can browse through the studio at his leisure, turning pictures aside to look behind them for stolen goods, taking off the lids of paint cans but careful to tap them firmly when he closes them. Or he might look at Suliman's work. This is interesting. This falls short. Colors are too harsh. The detective would have his tastes. He knows what Suliman does during the school day while she is ticking off the hours of the freedom that Kate begrudges him between seven and four o'clock.

"I'm here."

"About time. You let me drive that car, you'd be here twenty minutes sooner."

"I can't let you have my car. You don't have a license."
"Ain't too hard to get. Guns are harder."
"Guns?"
"Convicted felons can't get gun permits, but they didn't say nothing about a driver's license. I even got the book from Secretary of State. Studying up for the written test. Criminals can still drive cars."
"You said you were in juvenile detention."
"The other stuff never came up. I ain't got any secrets. You got a question, I'll give you the answer. But even before I got sent away, I could drive. Since I was eleven."
"Eleven-year-olds can't drive."
"They can't get a license, but I know a bunch of them been stealing cars since they could tie their shoes."

The afternoon has started on a sour note. Kate considers going home even though she will get caught in five o'clock traffic going to the West Side.

The detective will be eating a McDonald's or reading the *Free Press*, and he will be caught off guard by her unexpected departure.

"But you know, we need to go the hardware store. I need anchors for the shelves I put up. They ain't going to hold the way they are right now."
"The shelves should have been done by now."
"Overseer just got here."
"Suliman...."
"Kate, artists don't have schedules. You want to know where I've been, ask me. Instead you poke around, checking for footprints, peering in windows, looking for clues. You're like a private eye, hired to check me out. When I am not too aggravated, in my mind I see you sniffing around like an Indian scout following a trail."
"All right then, where have you been?"
"Downtown. On the bus. Looking around."
"For what?"
"I can look around, right? Or is that against the house rules?"
"I don't want to argue, Suliman."
"I don't start it. I am not an arguing man."

Suliman is not an arguing man. He is, in fact, compliant. There should be something more to what happens between people.

"It's okay," she says.
"What's okay?"
"That you don't love me."
"Love, now that's something I don't ever deal with. In fact, I don't have a clue what women mean when they start up about love."
"You loved your mother."
"Couldn't say. Can hardly remember her."

"A girl in school."

He laughs. "My school didn't have no girls in it, not when I could do anything about it."

Kate is silent when Suliman lets go bit by bit the facts of his life. He gives her a piece here and a piece there, and she waits for the next one.

"And when I got out of all the places they find to put me in, when I finally get out, it ain't love I was thinking about. It was the noise in the street, the door that opens to a restaurant and all those people sitting down at tables. It's fruit all arranged by color, orange and red. Limes. Bananas and apples and rosy peaches. Cans all neat in a row and boxes of cereal.

"In the beginning, I couldn't get enough of the supermarket. I would stand in the meat department just looking. You got your chicken, whole ones, cut-up pieces, breasts, thighs, wings. Then you got pork, roasts and chops, and you know the juices got to be fresh blood. Next there's all the beef. That's the biggest section.

"I have my supermarket dream. Maybe it's more like a daydream. I have a great big cart and a special book, like food stamps, only there ain't limits to what I can have. There's a food stamp for anything I want in that supermarket. Pop, candy, chocolate chip cookies, fancy napkins, magazines, a pineapple just because I feel like painting a picture of a pineapple.

"Love? It ain't on my list of real things. But I know what you're asking me about. What I feel. About you."

"That's right."

"You won't like it."

"I need to know."

"Well, you're good people, a little messed up because of your home life. Like me, you are hungry, but only for one thing. Okay, I can give you the one thing you think is so important because I'm grateful. For everything, for this gallery about to be happening.

"So if you want grateful and love to mean the same thing, it's okay with me. It comes out the same way. It ain't hard to make love with you. Sometimes I can see the pretty young girl in your face, and you're not fat or sloppy. So it's working out, leastways for me."

Kate's heart is an empty well. All she has to fill it with is gratitude.

"It works for me, too."

# Chapter Twenty-one: Mothering

There is a note on the kitchen table: "Call your daughter." Michael hasn't put the number on the note, but then he wouldn't. Three words. That's all he has to give her.

She calls on the cell phone. She isn't calling from the house and sharing her conversation with Michael. It is damp and cold in the garage. She is shivering. It has to be from the cold.

"Shannon?"

"Mom, is something going on?"

"The usual is going on."

"Dad says he never sees you."

"Isn't that what he wants?"

"No, Mom, he never sees you."

"That's right."

"Do you have someone?"

"Let's just say I have some place."

"Where is this place?"

"The same place where you are, Shannon. A place that isn't home, so it doesn't matter where it is."

"That isn't a satisfying answer, Mom."

"How are you, honey?"

"I'm making out. Things could be better, but they've been worse."

"Are you going to stay with him? There?"

"Probably not, but yes, for now. Until I know something."

"Something?"

"Anything. Like where to go next. So, do you have a number I can call, a cell or something?"

Kate gives Shannon the cell phone number. It has decided something. She has been leaving her cell phone with Suliman during the day. But now he can't be the one to answer it. She will have to get him a phone of his own. One more expense, but she isn't as concerned about money as she is about who Suliman will call when he has his own phone. She will have no record of his calls, the scroll she reads at stoplights when she is leaving Hamtramck and going back to Southfield, the numbers that she redials.

The voices are sleepy, black voices, sometimes men, sometimes women. She hangs up. She isn't worried about the black voices. The Fairlane Motel woman is the only one she is worried about. Because she understands her willingness to pay the bills, to keep a man on a chain, a golden chain so that he can't go very far.

She won't be able to check his calls, but she doesn't want another reason to be estranged from her daughter. It has been months since Shannon has called her.

"Girls, motherhood is the reason we get married. Write that down. Marriage equals motherhood. Doesn't that make sense? Historically. The family unit exists for the welfare of the children. We see it everywhere in nature. Mating and nurturing. Protection, too. The father is the protection. The mother is the nutrition." She conjures up the image of the male lion prowling before the mouth of the cave, the mother lion curling around the helpless cub. The girls must see it too, there is such a silence in the room, such a dreaminess.

"Let's take the lessons of nature and apply them to ourselves. We have all the ingredients to create a child. We just need to get the right mixture, the right consistency." The girls laugh softly, imagining the preparation of a cake or a mixing of muffin batter. "Isn't it safe to say that we have been put on earth for the business of creation?"

The girls nod in agreement.

"Well, then, where do you learn how to be a mother?"

"From reading books."

"You learn from your mother."

"Yes, from your mother. She is the role model for taking care of your child. She is in your memory. She will guide you through the first diaper change, the first bath, which is oh so scary, that tiny creature, the little arms and legs beating against the cold air, shocked by the first immersion into water, the first experience of soap."

"What if your mother isn't there?"

"What about orphans?"

"What if you grew up in day care?"

"It doesn't matter. Your mother is still there. You'll know it when the time comes."

She had not meant to drive Shannon away. She was trying to hold on because Shannon was the unexpected gift of marriage.

When Shannon referred to Kate as "mother," it was a title, preceding the complaints.

"My mother keeps me a prisoner. She wants me to work at Farmer Jack's or in a department store."

"My mother puts my school schedule on the refrigerator and calls the police if I am ten minutes late."

"My mother doesn't care if I attend a college. In fact, my mother would prefer it if I had a vocation. She would like me to became a nun even though we don't go to church. Someone will have the keys to lock up Shannon."

Kate had listened to Shannon's conversations on the kitchen phone. She had gone through Shannon's closet, her shoeboxes, her underwear drawers, folding and unfolding her sweaters, looking for a clue or a note, something to prove Kate's conviction that her daughter had a secret life.

Kate had accused her daughter in her thoughts. On her way home from middle school, Kate was positive, she stopped behind a garage where a boy fondled her. She washed away the smell of sex in a public bathroom in Burger King or at a gas station. Kate was convinced of this. The strict curfew did not stop her from lying in the back seat of a car, the boy covering her.

*"Girls, do you know where the word curfew comes from? From 'cover the fire.' When the fires were put out, it was time to go home."*

Cover the fire. Don't let your mother know about the burning that drives you from the house and gets you tangled up in the body of a boy in a place where there is only darkness and danger.

She knows the score, and she loves her daughter enough to limit the possibilities. You can't eliminate danger, but you can set up some barriers.

*"Protection, girls. Our first duties as mothers are basic: shelter, food, warmth, cleanliness. And protection because what else does that child have but her mother."*

"I don't need your permission to live, Mother," Shannon had said so many years ago, five now. "I can walk away. You can't stop me."

Suliman could walk away, too. He could be hungry and without a place to live, but if he were pressured too much, he would leave.

Michael stays because he hates her. He doesn't want her to forget it. She breathes it in every day. Her clothes reek of it. Her hair is oily with it. Poison has seeped into her pores.

# Chapter Twenty-two: Reasons For and Against

Suliman's reasons to stay must have more weight on the balance scale than his reasons to leave.

Reasons to Stay: Studio (rent), food (cooking), artist supplies (brushes, acrylics, watercolors, pens), cost of materials (rebuilding studio), appliances (stove, refrigerator, space heater for bathroom), companionship (sex).

Reasons to Go: Sex (age difference), money (too little), limitations (no car), privacy (lack of), confinement (other women), art (no new work), street life (black people).

She has already been accused of tyranny by her daughter and her husband. It is time to move the pieces around. Or he will leave.

Sex has the greatest weight. She will have to decide which scale it belongs on.

He wants a phone line. Long distance. "You know, when I get started, and dealers want to talk to me." She will stall about the long distance.

He hasn't been painting in the new studio.

"What are you thinking about, Suliman?" It has to be the other woman, the one from Dearborn. Or some young, light-skinned girl. Any woman who might see the fine, broad planes of his face, the perfect (delicious) curve of his mouth. Any woman would want a man whose body is silk over rock; she will lose him if she doesn't share him.

"I'm working on my vision. I see it, then it goes slipping away. Maybe if I went out a little more, it'll come to me. Take a little ride early in the morning, look at the city, like on my own. Take a sketch pad, some pencils. An artist can't just be sitting in a studio, coming up with stuff. He needs inspiration."

He could be talking about women and their sexiness when they know they are desirable. When you lose it, you are left with artifice.

The balance scales must tilt in a different way.

She will give him more spending money. He will have to consider what he stands to lose by leaving. She can't be stingy (as she has been about paints, poster board, canvas board, sketch pads, pens, charcoals, and those horribly expensive brushes, so many of them.)

"Now I see why artists starve," she had said in an artist supply store. "If this keeps up, we are both going to the poorhouse."

He had walked out of the store. She was shocked that he could walk away.

Time. She has to give him private time. Even though he is the only place where she wants to be.

"Ain't there something you want to do, Kate, that doesn't involve me? Not saying you aren't welcome. Not saying that. This place is more yours than mine. I was just wondering if you didn't have some interests that aren't happening here."

She could go to a library and read the newspaper or to the malls where there is nothing she wants. Waiting. She will have to do it. She can drive across the Ambassador Bridge to Windsor and go the bar at the River Hilton. She can drink double Scotches and watch the People Mover racing around the buildings, a few dark figures in the lighted cars. She can watch the river traffic and the afternoon turn into night. Then she can go home. The next day she might skip the morning or come later in the afternoon. She will tell him that she was busy.

The solitary time she has conjured is so vivid that she begins to cry. She can't do it; she can't stay away. She can't let him go to someone else, not so she knows.

He can get his driver's license. Then he can drive her to school and pick her up. That is killing two birds. That's weighting the scales sensibly. Not so sensibly. The car has a lot of miles, and the last thing she can afford is a new car.

He will drive everywhere. She will write down the number of miles, but there will be no way to know where he has gone. She is afraid, but there is nothing else she can do. There is no way to prevent what torments her so much: Suliman with someone else.

Suliman wants a phone listed in his name in the Yellow Pages: Al-Rashid, Suliman, Artist and Sculptor.

"I ain't living no more under a woman's name," he says.

"But you can live on a woman's money," she would like to say.

# Chapter Twenty-three: Waiting

Suliman is still bitter about the woman, Linda.

"Like what is the right thing to call a woman who keeps you locked up like a monkey in a cage? For sure, I didn't call her by her name." He says he called Linda "baby" and "sugar," and she had liked that. "You can tell she ain't had no black man before. Then she'd know that's what they call their women in case they forget their names."

Suliman can't forget Kate's name because he calls to her across the studio: to help him move a separating wall; to hand him some paint thinner when he is up on the scaffold painting the ceiling. She is the blind assistant to his vision.

"Look at this, Kate. This is my place. You're the best, girl. I never met a woman who works harder than you."

Kate is always tired. If someone asked her, she would say that she was happy. But there is no one she can tell about the studio, about the shared hours of work after school and on the weekends. About the smell of the paint and the mineral spirits, the quick lovemaking in the unmade bed, the days getting longer and the illusion of more available time. More time for work, more time for love, more time for being with Suliman.

Suliman is not painting. He is waiting, he says, to feel in his hands for the right moment.

"Right now we are making a place for the real thing, the real art of Suliman. It's floating around in my head, but it slips away just as I'm about to get my hands on it. Pretty soon it will come drifting down from the sky or wherever visions keep themselves until they find the right people."

Kate doesn't care about visions. She only cares about holding on.

She is skipping personal steps. She ties up her hair, gray showing at the roots because there isn't time for coloring her long hair. She will have it cut short the next chance she gets.

Wrinkled dresses lie on the floor of her closet. She doesn't have time to drop them by at the cleaners. She has to buy pantyhose at the all-night supermarket after she leaves the studio. She forgets to take earrings with her in the morning, or her watch.

She doesn't have the time for the complicated ritual of making a younger face.

She is in the teacher's lounge, buying a Coke and a candy bar from the vending machines. "Girl, you sick or something?" another teacher asks her.

"I'm on a diet," Kate says.

"Pretty good diet, Coke and candy. If it was me, I'd be weighing five hundred pounds."

Kate is burning up. She is a conflagration. The fire is Suliman; the fire is everything.

# Chapter Twenty-four: Intimations

Kate can see for herself, Suliman says, throwing back the sheet, that he has a body made for boxing. He was always hanging out at the gym. No one took any interest, he was just a kid, skipping school and not too serious about anything. But no denying he was strong and quick on his feet.

"Being a boxer for me was like other guys and basketball. Sure, someone is going to beat you big time, but no matter what, you end on top. You'll be the guy who got beat up by a big name, his fists hitting your face, his blood splattering all over you when you get a good one in. I didn't think I'd be on top. I just wanted to be in the game."

It wasn't about money, he said. Money was like water, slipping away. Even when he was young, he knew that.

"Hunger didn't mean nothing to me either because it always came back. You could eat and eat, but sure enough the next day, you're hungry again."

Money, clothes, sex, food. That's what everyone wanted at sixteen, seventeen. Not him so much. Sure, he liked to be cool with the right shoes and a jacket that someone would want to pull off his back. He didn't know about the artist waiting for the right time to take over and make him straight. There were only—what should he call them—hints. Intimations.

He remembered the word. One day he wandered into school because there was nothing to do, or it was cold. Or he wanted see what trouble he could stir up in class. The teacher was reading poetry. He rolled his eyes and smiled at his running buddies, slouching in the seats made for children. Like someone forgot that at seventeen, you are the man you are going to be. Grown, too big for the rooms and the seats and the lessons.

The teacher writes on the blackboard, "Intimations of Immortality." That didn't mean anything to him. He knew what immortal was. Like Superman except when he was around Kryptonite. And Jesus. But he wasn't Jesus or Superman.

"How do you know that you have an immortal soul?"

"I am saved," a girl said. "That's how I know."

"Yes, of course. Anyone else?" the teacher asked.

"The sun don't never burn out."

"Weeds. Talk about immortal. Every year they get a new lease on life."

"The ocean is always there. Rolling and rolling, the same every day."

"Yes, yes," the teacher said. "These are hints of forever." She looked like she was going to fall down on her knees and start praying. Instead she read the poem. He still remembers part of it:

*There was a time when meadow, grove, and stream*
*and every living thing did seem to be*
*Appareled in celestial life,*
*the beauty and the freshness of a dream.*

Then it slipped away from him, like everything. The words of the poem, like money, slipped away.

The day he learned about intimations, he took a gun in his hand as if something important were about to be revealed to him.

"I didn't know about my personal holiness then. Wish I learned it sooner, but you walk on the path chosen for you even if it means hurting other folks along the way. The bad thing is, it ain't easy to forget who you did wrong to along the way to finding out who you are. Guess maybe that's what they mean about seeing ghosts, the ghosts of your own bad deeds.

"I had to be in charge of that gun. We took somebody's car and drove to Pontiac. We figured that no one would know us there. Could have gone a mile and no one would know us, but we had our plans. We'd go on back to Detroit, stick the money under our mattress, and save it for a rainy day.

"We were kids. Couldn't think any farther than tying our shoes so we wouldn't trip while we're ripping off a supermarket at night."

He had it all planned: money coming out of people's wallets, going into the cash registers, and then into his pocket. The trouble was, there was a manager who saw them coming. They saw him, too. He pulled out the gun anyway.

"You look like a man, you act like a man."

Then he was in a jail cell without his buddies. Because the gun in his hand made the difference between the seventeen years of their lives and his seventeen years.

"I was a juvenile, but I shot a gun in a supermarket and hit a lady. Then I was an adult. Detective says lucky for me she only screamed like she was gonna die."

Then everything was like a dream. He didn't remember eating or who was in the cell with him. No one came forward for him. He was hoping maybe someone would read in the papers that Gary Johnson was arrested for attempted robbery and wounding a bystander in a Pontiac supermarket. Then his cousin or his aunt would come by.

"I must have looked like a big criminal to the judge. He didn't have one bit of mercy. Didn't even consider me a juvenile. Eight years. Like it's some magical number meant for me."

The other guys, he tells Kate, got sent to a juvenile home for eighteen months. That's where they belonged, because the moment the police came, "those little pussies started crying."

Then someone came for him, not a relative or a lawyer, but a preacher, a man of God, who took him from his cell and walked with Suliman right out the door into the light.

It was the first time that he had encountered an angel, one of the angels that hung around ordinary people, looking for the intimations of immortality. Yes, he would have to call it that.

"For a long time I always painted a black angel in every picture. The angel got smaller, but he was always there. It was my signature, saying thank you to Lester for saving me. He was the only one who saw that I wasn't nothing but a boy who didn't know to do any different."

# Chapter Twenty-five: Ellis Island

Lester Adams drove Suliman to the gate of Ellis Island.

"Boy," Lester said, "This is your chance for a new life. The people who created this place named it Ellis Island. Now I know you heard of it because I know you went to school. You probably thought Ellis Island was just a place for foreign folks looking to be free.

"Well, you are looking to be free, too. You need a new country just as bad as those folks from Europe. Nothing behind you and everything in front of you. If you got the will power and a personal dream, like those immigrants, you can be making yourself a new life."

Lester said that when the car door opened, he was a free person. He could walk away and disappear until the law found him. Or he could be a free man and open the gate to Ellis Island. There were no locks and no bars, only a fence to keep the horses in. He could give himself over, that's what Lester said, "Give yourself over to the process of becoming yourself."

The whole world was lying right under his feet, and there were places to hide. But there were no doors to open and no one to say, "Gary, come on in. We been waiting on you." No one was waiting for him except in this place with a weird name which wasn't an island or a prison or a school.

Lester said, "I don't want to know if you take your opportunity, or if you run. You make that decision after I drive away."

"Just like that, I'm a free man. My first thought is to run. But my feet don't go because my feet know what my head doesn't know. No place to run but in circles and end up back in The House of Correction."

He stood at the gate, feeling like a fool and afraid to go in. Then he laughed, thinking of other doors that had been closed to him—never mind locks and keys, he always got inside.

Then a guy rushed out, greeting him like he was some long-lost brother come home from the war. "You must be Gary," he said. "We hoped you would get here in time for lunch. We put a plate aside for you."

Suliman—then he was Gary—could not recall a time when someone put aside food for him. All he can remember is his granny saying, "Boy, you can't get here when the food is on the table, you ain't doing any eating."

The white guy smiled like some kind of lunatic when Suliman told him that he had a history of missing meals. He surprised himself because he couldn't remember making conversation except when he wanted to get beside some girl. Making polite conversation with a white man was something new for him.

Suliman was hungry. And he knew that once you took a man's food, he had the right to ask something of you.

He ate his lunch with his brotherhood. Only he didn't know that these people were his brotherhood, his group.

He didn't speak at lunch because for the first time in his life he felt fear. "I ain't saying I was never afraid. Waking up you'd be stupid not to be afraid. But that don't stop you. Day goes by, maybe something bad happens or nothing happens. Being afraid is what you can live with. Then a door opens and closes behind you." That first day at Ellis Island the door opened wider than he had ever seen it before. "Like the light folks say they see when they pass over, that's the kind of light that came pouring through that door."

Napkins were folded under the plastic forks and knives. The spoons were standing up like flowers in a cup in the center of the table. There was soup, and he ate it even though the taste of canned tomato soup reminded him of juvenile and shelters and soup kitchens. "From when I was small, you know. When life wasn't so regular." Now there was a regular lunch: sandwiches and Kool-Aid and a plate of cookies.

"Talk about clockwork, that's when you ate at Ellis Island. By the clock. Seven o'clock, but you better take your shower first. Twelve thirty for lunch, and don't even think about sneaking out before the book review. Dinner at six thirty, and you dress for it, like school boys, wearing white shirts, neckties, and khakis.

"The person in charge, you always know who he is. Only the person in charge of us wasn't a man. It was Karen. She didn't need a badge or keys rattling from a chain to let you know. It was just who she was. The person in charge. In charge of herself."

"Gary will be taking Kenny's spot," Karen said. "Duane, you will show Gary where he will be living."

"I got to thank you, man," Duane said, "for getting me out of book reports. Just when you think to take you a little nap, you gotta snap right awake and listen to some fool talk about the book he read. A course, won't no one read a book if they didn't get a free fifteen minutes. I got forty-five minutes saved up, but I'm waiting for something important to show up 'fore I use my time."

"Ain't nothing worth reading a book for," he said to Duane, but he didn't mean it; he was sorry that it was the first thing that he said to Duane.

"It ain't so bad when you get into it," Duane said, sizing up Suliman. "I guess you kinda big through the shoulders. Almost an extra large."

"I been in training. To be a fighter. So what happened to this Kenny?"

"Got sent back," Duane said, shaking his head. "Not that it wasn't obvious from the get-go. Kenny could not get with the program. Every morning, someone say to him, 'Kenny, you got to turn yourself around.' And Kenny would look so sad, like he knew he wasn't ever going to be able to do it. No matter what."

It was bad luck to fill Kenny's spot. He didn't want to know any more.

"Okay," Duane said, "you entitled to two pair of khakis, a sweater, a sweat shirt, and some t-shirts. Shoes, and they new until you make them old. Underwear. Ain't no shortage of underwear, so don't go wearing out the same pair of socks or nothing like that. You want to go to worship, you request your church clothes. And don't be keeping the good things to yourself. You want to sleep in pjs, that's cool. Only no sleeping in the raw, don't even ask me why."

Suliman never had a pair of pajamas, not that he could remember. He was sure that he would fling them aside in the night.

He took a long time arranging his clothes and making his bed. "We do it Army style," said Duane, "tight and neat. We get a good inspection, that's ten free minutes. Bad inspection is negative ten. Everybody be pissed if we get a bad inspection.

"Karen say you suppose to take a rest until dinner. Now this is a real privilege, and don't be expecting it like it's your right. Around here, it's work from before breakfast until dinner chores is done. But she say that you need to have a fresh start."

There were voices and the slanting light of afternoon. Then he slept.

# Chapter Twenty-six: The People in Charge

"We aren't as relentless as God," Gerald said, "but we are vigilant."

Gerald was the one who stayed clean and straight so long that he didn't remember being someone else. But he wasn't the kind of man to preach before you got yourself together.

"The ancients understood that you feed the hungry wayfarer first. You let him rest. Then you ask him questions." Gerald was good with words because he took up reading when his mind got straight.

"Adam and Eve lose Eden forever for breaking the rules. At Ellis Island you have your first second chance at life.

"We don't wear blue jeans here," Gerald said. "Denim was created to clothe the disenfranchised workers. By the French, in De Nimes."

"Like I cared, but funny thing is that I always remember Gerald saying that about denim."

Suliman could see that Gerald was a man who knew his worth. He had been around, but whatever had happened was called the past, and he wasn't walking that way again.

Gerald took him on the tour. The dining room, the kitchen, the walk-in pantries stacked with big cans of fruits and vegetables, the unmarked sacks of government surplus; the icy walk-in refrigerators with frozen blocks of hamburger meat and slabs of cheese. In the common rooms there were couches big enough to put up your feet and stretch out and big, slouchy chairs. Only no one was sitting around. He wanted to ask where the swimming pool was, but Gerald was a serious guy.

"This is the work area," Gerald said while they were walking down a long corridor away from the lounge. "Everyone gets a chance to work in every area here at the Island. It's how we support ourselves."

Thing was, Gerald wasn't wearing clothes that were any better than the people working in the kitchen, in the furniture studio, or in the painting studio. His clothes were dusty from unloading the unpainted urns and vases and planters. There was dirt under his fingernails and creases of dark sun on his face.

"Discipline," Gerald said. "There should be a softer word for it. What makes us do what we have to in order to satisfy ourselves."

They were standing in the room where men, not all of them young, were holding up white vases to the light to see the design, then lowering their heads to dip the brushes into their pots of paint. Peace and dissatisfaction, mixing together.

"Passion," Gerald said. "Not the passion of the moment, but the force that rises up and sustains you. Through everything. Passion. It makes men into gods."

Suliman had been tricked by Lester. The people running the place were crazy with some kind of religion. That had to be the tremor, the rippling, that he felt under the surface of busy-ness and purpose: people dropping seedlings into the pockets of dirt in planters; the steady hum of the lathe in the furniture studio; the bent heads over sewing machines, hemming curtains and bedspreads.

"On the other side of the barn is the auto shop. Every car we have here at the Island came to us as a piece of junk. You learn a lot undoing the damage of time and neglect. But you'll see. When it's your turn to do auto."

"I ain't mechanical."

"How do you know what you are?"

Is that what he had said? Or was it something more ordinary. Like experience is the best teacher. Or you will find out what you are good at. But what he meant is what is remembered. How do you know what you are?

"One time I tried to paint a picture of Ellis Island. Never tried to do it again because there are some things that can't get put down, but the Island will follow me around until I'm six feet under.

"I didn't have the experience of prison to see that the Island was somebody's dream come true. I was seventeen years old and been running wild all my life. Wild was the only thing I knew. Wild was what I was yearning for.

"Every night, ten o'clock, meetings started out quiet with maybe a few complaints like someone overslept, left a book out in the library, wouldn't change a channel, stuff like that. Then, boom, whoever was out to get you raised his head like a snake and struck.

"Even if you'd been scrubbing pots all day and setting tables and washing floors, and all you want is to go to sleep, forget it. You had to attend the brotherhood meeting. And every single thing you did that day or the day before, every flicker passing across your face, like maybe you didn't like the breakfast cereal or getting assigned to general labor, somebody was watching you and storing it up for brotherhood meetings with the twelve people who lived together and ate together and turned each other inside out like airing out a room.

"You know, the people who thought up Ellis Island, straight people, not like Gerald and Karen, they must have believed that everyone wanted to be straight like them: wake up in the morning and know what they had to do, which would be the same thing as what they wanted to do. Then it's dinnertime and they sit down at a nice hour like six o'clock and the napkin is in the right place and no spots on the drinking glasses. Big plates of meat and hot gravy for the mashed potatoes. And they'd think to themselves that they had made a success of things. They had created an enterprise that did good for people who couldn't get it together."

The Island was someone's dream, and in this dream there were bungalows and gardens and doors that never got locked. The main house was a little run-down, but Suliman could see the signs of the rich people who donated it, probably because their consciences were bothering them for being lucky.

"The straight people, they left because Ellis Island wasn't about being straight; it was about learning the rules of straightness. Celia and Tom, the founders, were pictures on the wall in the dining room. They're probably living somewhere in a nice little house, clinking their glasses together, filled with Diet Pepsi. They could have a mansion, and nobody would say they didn't deserve it. 'Well, dear, we did it. Reclaimed all those people.' And they wouldn't be bragging. They'd just be feeling good about themselves.

"Sure, they'd be thinking about the lost ones, the wild ones, but it wouldn't cross their minds that some people want to be free and aren't afraid of what that means. Nine to five is a state of mind you're born with. It's nothing you can learn. Gerald and Karen learned to be nine to five people so they could fight the junkies inside of them. They were never slipping backward."

He knew that, given a chance, any one of his group members would get high for at least a week without thinking twice. Even though the gate would close with them on the wrong side of it.

"I never had a problem with drinking or substances, you know what I mean, but I do know a lot of guys, women, too, who cannot live without the stuff and spend every waking minute trying not to use. Man, it becomes the meaning of their lives. Keep me away from those reformed addicts because they got eyes like searchlights, looking, looking, looking for your addiction. So they can sweep you in and make you straight.

"Karen and Gerald, they had those searchlight eyes, and they had something else. Invisible chains holding them in, keeping them from spilling out, running like a river in all kinds of directions. Wild. Like they are.

"One day I was looking at Karen. She was sitting at her desk, making her big decisions. The woman was concentrating so hard and most likely she was only writing a note to herself about someone who is starting to slip, the girl who is showing too much skin and the guy she is showing it to likes it too much. Something like that.

"Karen was tall and straight, no bumps and lumps. Like a model. And I could see her in a black dress with skinny straps and some high heel shoes. She would be a knockout. But if she put on something like that, she would feel like her flesh was on fire. She'd rip off that dress because the woman she was keeping under cover wasn't ever coming out again.

"'No,' I said to myself, but I didn't know what I was thinking. Now I do, but I wasn't entitled.

"Karen wore straightness like work clothes, and she never took them off. She had found her power. She gathered it to herself. She never slipped, but then I wasn't inside her dreams, the ones that went skittering and sliding through her head at night when she was sleeping in her own little room that was the reward for gathering up your power.

"So here I was, sleeping in a dorm with a bunch of other guys, not that I been sleeping alone my whole life. But this was orderly sleeping. Some guys wore their underwear, better be sure it was clean, some in their pj's, looking like fags, me included. Nobody's talking to each other because it is not a normal thing for grown men to be sleeping like this. Unless they're in the army or in a shelter, but that ain't normal either.

"There were times in my life when I would fall asleep wherever I was standing. Not washing, no blanket and, for sure, no pj's. The lights might be shining in my face or it could be morning, ten or eleven o'clock. Thing is, there wasn't a pattern. There was just the chance to sleep.

"Lying there waiting for sleep to come on a schedule was the worst thing for me. The rest of it I didn't mind. I could cooperate. Show up on time for breakfast set-ups, dishwashing, hauling crates, emptying garbage. The kind of stuff you had to do to prove you could 'Live Communally.' Not like being a communist, mind. No, it was about finding yourself by giving up your self. If that makes any sense.

"Gerald called me aside one day. Guess I was looking unhappy because there was no end to the ways they thought of testing the New Arrivals. Only thing was, I didn't feel unhappy. I was leaning on a shovel, about to turn up the ground in the garden, and I was thinking about growing things. Deeply thinking.

"He touched me on the shoulder, a little more than a tap but nothing you could misunderstand. Fatherly, you know, but with a lot more authority. 'You will see when you get to the other side'—like I am about to cross the River Jordan—'that all of this is for the good of your immortal soul, the true force of your being. The soul demands rigor; it thrives on order.' 'I ain't complaining,' I said. But maybe he could see that I was turning away from the idea of Ellis Island."

Suliman's first after-lunch book review was about the Tuskegee Airmen. "You might like this, Gary. If you feel self-conscious about giving the report, you can practice during the meeting the night before."

He told Ralph, the guy in charge of books, that he thought he had forgotten how to read. Ralph laughed and said that it was like riding a bicycle. "I ain't never rode no bike," he said, but it wasn't true. Any bike he had ridden, he had stolen and flung aside after a short, uneven flight.

Before he left Ellis Island, he gave four book reports. He saw that reading was easier than riding a bike because it carried you along without any real effort. He liked it. The quiet library felt like a church, books up to the ceiling so that you had to climb a ladder to get to certain parts of the alphabet. Sitting in an armchair reading a book, no one said that you were slacking off. Reading was a legitimate activity at Ellis Island.

What he didn't like was talking in front of white people.

"That was the first time I ever heard myself speaking. Made me wonder, what could people be thinking when I opened my mouth and all those put-together sounds come rolling out? For sure a lot didn't make any sense."

He didn't feel grateful for the bed with a good mattress, or the wardrobe for his clothing, or the lamp on a little nightstand. "You know, for keeping your book and maybe a glass of water." He had been tied up with a million strings like that guy Gulliver when he got captured by the little people. He wanted to shake off the rules, the endless Ellis Island rules that sounded like privileges, but each one was a link of the chain he had to wear until his head bowed beneath the weight of the rules.

"When you obeyed all the rules, you got the freedom to stay. That didn't make sense to me. I was already there. How come I needed the freedom to stay?"

If he had gone to prison first, he wasn't talking about jail or juvenile because that's a whole different matter, he would have known that Ellis Island was as good as it could get. It was better even than freedom because Ellis Island was about getting straight with yourself. That's all you needed to live. Not God or money or love. Just the assurance that your two feet are enough to stand in the world and your two hands can make something to be proud of.

All the steadiness was turned upside down at night at the group meetings. Turned upside down and inside out. All the bad things about you got laid out on the table, and there was no hiding them.

Group sessions had to be something a white person thought up. Let it all hang out. Scream and yell and tell people that you don't like their attitude. He couldn't ever do it, yell back, cry, whatever they wanted even when his face got rubbed into it. For being a punk and a thief and a liar and a thug. For heading right toward Death Row where his kind belonged since the day he was born. For ignoring his God-given right to be human and splendid. He didn't know what they were talking about, probably nothing, a bunch of ex-addicts, potheads, winos, sniffing glue from a bag. Whatever they could get.

But then there was the peacefulness of the work assignment. You paid your dues: thirty days in the kitchen from six in the morning until eight at night when the stoves are shining like jewels. Then you got your assignment, which didn't depend on who you were, but what was needed.

He was assigned to the woodshop: the lathes and the chisels, the stains and the shellac. Three months and the smell of wood. "Headboards and mirror frames, hair brushes, stuff like that. Nightstands sometimes. It depended on the orders. Simple furniture. I liked it, the smell of wood and all, but then I had to go to ceramics and do the planters. The rule of Ellis Island: No staying in one place."

# Chapter Twenty-seven: Group Session

He is the victim of his own crimes. Pretty soon a man could be whipping himself for his thoughts, never mind his little acts of badness.

He is caught for thinking nasty, for the way his eyes travel when Karen comes into the room. He likes to look at her, and whatever he is thinking, he doesn't have the pictures for it. For sure, it isn't what they said. It is soft and gentle, but it passes across his face as if it were desire. And someone is watching.

He can't believe they are talking about him.

"The guy looked at her like she was parading around in the altogether."

"Karen? You got to be shitting me. That don't show respect."

"What you got to say for yourself, Gary? Think you're good enough to touch her fingernail?"

"She is an angel and he is looking at her like she is a whore."

"Think those pretty-boy looks are going to get you some snatch?"

"Better get acquainted with your hand before you think about touching one hair on Karen's head."

"Bet you got a lot on the outside, didn't you, Gary? Pretending to be innocent. You guys know anyone who is innocent of anything? Any-thing?"

"Maybe Jesus."

"Even Jesus knew temptation, but this Gary, he probably thinks temptation means something he ought to do."

"Like fuck Karen."

"With his little dick."

"Oh, you seen it in the shower?"

"Too small to see."

"You know, Gary, you are exactly the kind of punk they're waiting for in prison. Where you definitely belong. Personally, you got all the characteristics of a permanent convict."

After that, he can't do anything but think of Karen as he would any woman. They thought they were bringing him down, but she is the one they broke into pieces.

She will see what is in his face when she looks at him. She will lean over to Gerald and tell him what is being telegraphed across the room. Then Gerald's eyes will turn to ice.

Karen and Gerald, they soar like fierce angels with fiery wings above the sleeping boys, the men, the girls, the ones saved from alleys and streets. Their eyes meet, satisfying everything. Then they sweep down in an ecstasy of fire, joined in the flame of their angel selves.

Gerald will keep his icy, human eyes on Suliman and freeze him out.

One morning—he doesn't even know he is going to do it—he walks to the gate and looks out at the road. He hears his own voice say: "Open the gate. Walk away."

He wished someone had seen him and yelled out, "Hey Gary, where are you going?" He will never know whether he would have turned back or if he would have run.

"Wasn't three days before I was arrested and no two ways about it, got the prison sentence that sounded like forever. Eight years. A rock rolled over my heart and stayed there the longest time.

"Everyone is pretty surprised because when I get to tell my story, folks think that the Island was where I found out I was an artist. But I got a theory that you are backed into your art. That it doesn't occur to you until there is nothing left to get your attention. Art is the last stop, and people are getting off the train too soon.

"Real prison brought me to art. The first picture I painted, a water color with the paleness of the green of growing things, was the garden, the earth turned up every day like I wanted it, the green of vines spilling over each other, the blooms that came up as flowers before becoming what they were meant to be, pushing out in a wash of green. I called it 'God's World' even though I am not one to conversate about God. But it's Ellis Island."

# Chapter Twenty-eight: Cable Connection

Kate is buying a television. She is looking for the cheapest set at ABC Warehouse. She hopes the salesman will give her a deal on his end because Suliman will want cable.

"It's something I got used to at the motel. A man can't be painting all day, no matter what the overseer thinks."

He calls her the overseer more than he says her name.

"You gotta take it yourself, lady," the salesman says. "We don't have delivery service. That's how come it's so reasonable."

She doesn't think it's reasonable. It is $600—"and this one will last forever"—but Kate doesn't believe in forever.

Suliman is on the phone. "You best speak to the lady of the house. She got the say-so, all the credit. Here she is."

"Basic cable or expanded? Platinum Tier is $97 a month, but you get every channel."

"No, no, basic is fine," Kate says.

"Don't basic mean bare bones?" He says sullenly. "Bare bones, bare floors, bare walls. Don't give your man nothing. This ain't any different than the motel. Just more room to put nothing."

The sales representative says, "You can go with Silver Tier. You get three premium packages."

"Silver is fine." She turns to Suliman. "Is there anything else you want?"

"You don't need to be so sarcastic. It kinda spoils the gift."

# Chapter Twenty-nine: Riding the Bus

She has gotten to the studio, and he is not there. She opens the cupboards and the laundry hamper. Has he been painting? She touches a canvas to see if it has been worked on, but it is dry. She has never seen him in the act of painting.

She is standing alone in Suliman's dream studio, which he leaves every day and to which he returns later and later each day.

She won't question him. He will say, "I don't need this. Can't pay the price."

She can't pay the price either. She should be the one to do the walking. Let him find the money for the perfect studio where everything is ready for the beginning.

She needs something to drink, but there is no alcohol in the studio. He doesn't need to drink the expensive Scotch he orders so freely when they go to a restaurant. That will have to come to an end, the eating out, the drinks, the movies. With her and without her. Because where can he go while she is working if he is not with a woman?

Anything he does without her is betrayal.

Six o'clock. "Suliman, it is six o'clock. Two hours since I got here."

"You know your way around."

"Please do not use that tone of voice with me."

"Sorry, Mrs. School Teacher, for being tardy."

"When I get here...."

"The slave got to be in attendance."

"You are an artist. An artist has to work."

"On your time schedule."

"On somebody's schedule."

"I am working. I'm riding the bus. I'm seeing the sights. Then I'm walking on the streets, looking at the details. And that ain't all. I am filling my soul with the city. I am drinking it up, swallowing it piece by piece."

"I am supposed to believe this."

"Whatever you want to believe is fine with me, but that is what I am doing. And, for sure, I am not showing any proof. Wait, maybe I can. You know, bring you back some transfers, a bus schedule, old newspaper I found on the seat of the Hamilton line. Then maybe you'd be happy. Then you'd get off my case."

"This is your studio. We worked so hard so that you can paint."

"Kate, an artist don't just wave a brush at a canvas. Something has to be there, and it's coming. The art of Suliman. And it ain't the kind of thing you can order up like a pizza or put together like a puzzle. It comes when it's ready."

"But riding the bus...."

"That's right, I'm riding the bus. First time, all I got is the newspaper and no pencil. I have been going out all my life with no paper and no pencil. Then I ask the guy next to me, 'You got anything to write with?' Cat says to me that he didn't have any plans to write a novel and get back with him tomorrow. I'll say this about riding the bus, everyone is crazy or plain city-angry.

"So, okay, I can deal. I pull the cord and get off the bus. Lucky for me I'm on Woodward, so there are some signs of life. Corner of Woodward and Warren is an art store. I go in, take out my little 'allowance,' which I don't need to tell you doesn't amount to anything after bus fare and a cup a coffee.

"'I need some supplies,' I tell the guy who doesn't look like he knows anything except how to ring up a cash register. But he turns out to be okay and gives me a deal on a sketchpad and some chalk. I could have used some felt tip pens, but you don't start bargaining with someone who has just given you his best deal.

"Wouldn't you know, I forgot to get a transfer when I got off that bus. I could have traveled all day with a couple of transfers under my belt. It doesn't matter where you are in the city, there are surprises on every street.

"So I walk. It's bone-ass cold. But there's a sun, icy but bright, flickering on the broken windows.

"One day, I am going to paint a mural two blocks long and two stories high. And I ain't worried about finding the space because everywhere I go, I see buildings big as fortresses, and the windows are like eye sockets, all blank and dark. So dark that it stops your eyes from seeing what you know is inside: dead leaves, glass, paper turning into something wet and alive, broken chairs, brown stains of water leaking down. Maybe birds. Rats for sure.

"One guy told me, he used to be a security guard downtown at National Bank, that rats are organized. Bang, it's midnight and they're out there, lining up like Roman soldiers in the movies. These rats, they're sitting up on the walls, on the fences, on the window ledges. Nobody knows where they've been all day. But after midnight here come the Kings of the Streets, sweeping over them. Nothing stands in their way.

"Because no one is out in the city, day or night. Everybody is hiding like rats do in the day.

"So what am I doing, riding the bus? I am amazing myself with beauty. For every burned-up house next door there's a house that's standing proud. I'm seeing everything two ways: the way it is and the way it was. Like on Alexandrine, it must have been a fine street back in the day. Folks build themselves some mansions. I walked past a house better than a palace.

"Right next door there is half a house looking like the fire was put out last night. I can smell the wood burning. Kids probably put a match to it after they got tired of running through it, pissing on the floor, breaking everything that's still whole. They shoot it up, chop it up, kick it in, all depending on their mood and what's in their hands. They don't know they're kicking down history and memory and dreams.

"In my mural, I am going to dream back the city. Starting with the art museum glowing with special light, so you know that it is a temple, I'm building the city back up from the ground. Those houses will shine. The bricks will be colors of red and brown. The shingles on the roofs will be green or burnt orange. Those falling down chimneys will be painted right back up so some smoke can come up from the fireplaces.

"Porches will be swept clean. White curtains will be hanging in the windows.

"And all around my city, green from the sweet rain falling, and those little yellow flowers peeping out, saying, 'Hey, we're still alive. We've only been sleeping.'

"Just so you know, Kate, I need to be taking some photographs."

"Photographs."

"See, here's my idea. There's a good camera, a 35-millimeter, in the pawnshop down the way. Guy's selling me a Polaroid for ten dollars, but the film costs an arm and a leg. But I need the 35-millimeter because of the detail, you know. So Polaroid is sort of like an outline, the other camera for filling in."

"Suliman."

"I ain't asking. I'm telling."

"There isn't an end to what you need. But I am getting to the end of what I can do."

"You know, you got it wrong. You're thinking, 'Suliman, he wants this, Suliman, he wants that. He's wringing me dry.' But I figure we're partners, so leastways I can tell you.

"I'm not asking for money. I can sell my paintings. Don't really want to. I planned to paint over them. I'm thinking, maybe I need a fresh start, you know, like a new subject. So this guy says he'll take all these lions and weeping mamas and little pickaninnies off my hands. Says he can sell them. Lot of folks think Africa means something to them. So he's giving me five-six hundred dollars. I don't want to think about his profit, but I ain't got time for hustling stuff I don't believe in any more."

"Because now you want to be a photographer."

"No, I do not want to be a photographer. I want to be a painter of the city. But, according to my calculations, a man painting in the middle of Fort Street or Michigan Avenue ain't living long."

"Artists do it all the time. Take photographs and paint from them. The camera, it gets what's there. An artist he gets what's living inside."

"It's always something."

"I do believe you said you would do anything to be a part of my dream."

"You know, Suliman, it might not look that way to you, but the well is empty."

"I didn't ask for nothing. I have my ideas and my dreams, but I didn't come begging."

"The money I pour into rent, materials, supplies, food. And now this business about photography."

"I need to take pictures of the city."

"Detroit? Have you been sleeping on those bus rides? There is no city."

"I guess you should be going now, Kate. Because I don't need to have this argument with you. I am an artist, and I got my vision. I don't need to be put down because you're having a fit of stinginess."

"In a very great manner of speaking, Suliman, I can decide to leave the place I pay for. In a manner of speaking, everything you have is mine."

"That's the truth, Miss Kate, but you only own the things. You don't own the artist."

# Chapter Thirty: Mending

"Girls, don't make the error of throwing away a worn-out tablecloth or a sheet that has gotten thin from washing. These things can still be useful. For example, you can embroider a pattern over the worn area of that tablecloth. Scatter the pattern, flowers or stars randomly, and before you know it, you have a work of art. Don't laugh, girls, not until you have examined all the creative possibilities of mending.

"The shabby sheet. Dye it with All-Purpose Rit, a dark color, purple, blue, even red, and you have something to work with. Of course, you had better give that washing machine a good rinse in vinegar, two cycles to get the color out." The girls write down, All-Purpose Rit and vinegar as if they have been given a recipe.

"If the sheet is a king-size, you can cut it in half. Stitch the edges up on your sewing machine, and you have two top sheets. Or you can make yourself a set of new pillowcases. Or a swag to cover that dull cornice board that came with the house." The girls write down "cornice," and she wonders how they will spell it.

"Cornice," she repeats. "It covers the rods and the curtain hooks. The old fashioned kind is usually covered with material that matches the draperies. I have always found them to be ugly and prefer the swag. It has a softer look and presents more decorative possibilities.

"Those sweaters with the stitches pulled out? Pull those unsightly threads to the inside with a crochet hook. A bleach spot on a skirt? Magic marker.

"We have forgotten about mending. It's easier to buy something new than to fix what's old and slightly worn. It's not about saving money; although, I am not going to pretend that money is not important. We have spent too much time talking about budgeting to forget about thrift. What I am talking about is valuing what we have. We throw too much away. We have not respected the service of a garment or an appliance or a piece of furniture.

"Let's try to be more thoughtful about what we have."

Kate will go home and make dinner for Michael. She will set the dining room table, using the best tablecloth and the linen and lace napkins. She will wash two crystal champagne glasses in warm, soapy water. They must be dusty.

She will get steaks, fillets; those little purple potatoes that cost so much; asparagus even though it's out of season. No time for a pie even if she buys a prepared crust. Two bottles of wine. Pouilly Fuisée. So expensive. But there is so much to mend.

It's late, and there are no fillets, so she chooses strip steaks. It would be a waste of money to buy fingerling potatoes. She can pop some russets into the microwave. The asparagus is too expensive. Green beans then, steamed. Just barely. She chooses a chardonnay. The Pouilly Fuisée costs too much.

The house is dark. She will set the table and be ready to cook when he comes in. Broiling, steaming, microwaving. It will take ten minutes at the most—as soon as she hears the garage door rumble open.

She meets him at the door.

"Michael. I haven't been coming home because I wanted you to...to be free because we...well, you know how it has been. But I'm here now. There's dinner and wine. We can talk. We can mend our fences."

"I'll eat with you, Kate. There are things to talk about."

"Has Shannon called you? Is she all right?"

"She's fine. At least she's escaped this."

"Escaped?"

"The claustrophobia of this house, the rules, the spying."

"I didn't spy on her. I was protecting her." From men on buses who heard her whispering, wavering heart, her obscene heart. From driving home at dawn with her stockings and underwear on the seat beside her.

"And I didn't spy on you, Michael."

"You didn't have to. I marched to your orders."

They sit at the kitchen table, not at the dining room table for the special meal even though they both know that she has cut corners.

"I have steaks."

"Fine."

"The meat cutters were gone. I couldn't get...."

"Whatever you have is fine."

"If I could know, Michael, what went wrong, well, I would feel better."

"Since when have you been concerned with feeling, Kate? Isn't appearance what you are all about?"

"All right then. Perhaps we could make a better appearance."

"I assume that you don't like the present arrangement."

"I don't understand it. Our life together simply stopped."

"You wrote the script, but you forgot to put in my lines. I was the silent partner in the story of Kate Mackey, Part Two. The sequel. Girl loses looks, decides to become respectable and marries."

"What are you talking about?"

"I am talking about you."

"Michael, I bailed you out of your life. Then you ran out of gratitude and all you have left is anger. Oh, don't let me forget about fear. A man who has failed as much as you have must be terribly afraid. Tiptoeing around in a house you didn't buy. Driving a car you couldn't finance. But that's not the worst of it. Turning Shannon away from me. The child you didn't want."

"The old grudge, Kate."

"Grudge? I don't think that word is strong enough." She gets up so quickly that she overturns her chair. "Let me look it up in the dictionary. Let's see if 'grudge' is a word strong enough for what I am feeling right now."

"It's been a pleasure dining with you."

"Get out of my house, Michael."

"I will. When you change the locks."

"I'm telling you."

"Not good enough, Kate. Words aren't good enough. They are just smokescreens. When the smoke clears away, it is pretty clear to me that I don't have to leave. Not because I am a coward. I am. But you are a coward, too. Two cowards share a house, a new definition of hell."

She is left in the kitchen. The steaks are curling up on the grill pan, the beans growing limp in the steamer. And she has opened the bottle of chardonnay, which means that someone will have to drink it.

# Chapter Thirty-one: History of a Marriage

"*Girls, show your best in everything. Put out your finest for guests, your friends, the unexpected visitor. Serve the coffee on a tray. Even if those china cups don't match, drinking coffee in a china cup becomes an experience to remember long after the caffeine wears off. Don't forget the little cloth napkins. You can refresh them in the dryer with a sheet of Bounce before using them.*

"*Use your best dishes for all occasions, even a family dinner. Dip the silver serving utensils in a liquid cleaner, rinse them in soapy water, and meat loaf becomes a gourmet dish.*"

How will the girls spell "gourmet"?

"*We want to be remembered, not for the things that have gone wrong, but for the little touches we were gracious enough to provide. Our courtesy in small things comes with big rewards, I promise you.*"

She had met Michael at a conference for Home Economics teachers. He was assistant vice president of marketing at a department store and the guest speaker.

The conference was held at the Hilton, three nights and four days. Dinners and cocktail parties supplied by vendors and publishers of textbooks.

She never shared a room. You couldn't tell what might come your way. If there was no one, then there was Northland Mall, the Northland Cinema, or the dark bar in the lobby when the cocktail party faded out.

This time there was Michael, slight but handsome, hair that had turned gray early and deep blue eyes. His suit fit him well. Casey wore suits that were custom made, but he still looked like a longshoreman.

Michael spoke well. The women in the room, all women of course, it was Home Economics, smiled at each other. So good looking.

In her room, the room at the Hilton that was not shared, and Casey was dying or already dead, Michael sat on the loveseat balancing his Scotch and water. Kate took a bottle of Cutty Sark whenever she went to a conference. And two glasses.

"You didn't get these glasses from the bathroom," he said.

"I like company. I plan for it. And these are my special glasses."

"Special?"

"For celebrations. It's a family custom."

"What are we celebrating?"

"Us."

"I've married everyone I've gone to bed with," he said.

"Good."

The wedding announcement is a statement. "Kate Mackey is marrying Michael Connally on Sunday at ten o'clock at Marygrove College. The Small Chapel, December 18, 1972. No gifts."

She has sent separate notes with the invitations. "We have everything, each other and our household goods. However, our refrigerator is gasping its last breath."

She doesn't tell Michael about the notes.

*How many times had she admonished the girls, while they were writing in their notebooks with Snoopy on the cover or Scooby Doo or Barbie, that asking for a specific gift is in bad taste? She walks around the room to make sure they get it right.* "Bad taste to ask for gifts." *She taps her pencil on her desk.*

"That's what Hudson's is for. To register your needs for all to see. People don't need to buy the gift at Hudson's if it is out of range of the household budget. But you have let people know—in a proper way, of course—about the saucepans, the deep fryer, the dishes you have chosen to accompany your life."

"Isn't registering the same as asking?"

"It's a list, not a demand. And if you don't register, you will get twelve sets of candlesticks that you might not be able to return."

*The girls laugh. They rarely do. She has stirred their deepest concerns that they will fail at housekeeping, child raising, grocery shopping, meal preparation, budget constraints, keeping a husband once they get him. Or they are indifferent, just wanting the credit for an elective course in order to graduate.*

Saul from the apartment across the hall—there had been a night—sent $100. Carol and Pete, $50, but they were new parents with a late child. Her brother, $200 and a note. "Sorry I couldn't make the wedding."

"These checks," Michael said. "I thought we specified no gifts."

"Oh, you know people."

He should have been grateful. She made the down payment on the house, settled his debts, managed his child support.

She was fooled in everything. The Catholic husband with three previous marriages, eight children, only two over eighteen and off the payroll. A studio apartment downtown in Lafayette Plaza, one room for everything he owned. Assistant vice president of not much of anything, always for a year or two and then somewhere else. Trained? "For nothing I can think of."

# Chapter Thirty-two: Waste

She takes the uneaten dinner to the studio: steaks, beans, potatoes, the loaf of French bread she had thrown into her basket at the last minute in the supermarket. The chardonnay, eight dollars, nine? She could throw it out. But then Suliman won't ask about the opened bottle.

He says he doesn't know how to use a corkscrew. She doesn't believe him. There is nothing about Suliman that she believes.

At the studio, the photographs are tacked to corkboards lined up against the walls. Suliman is quick to explain.

"Glad I'm rid of that excuse I was calling art. Those paintings were nothing but a waste of paint and canvas.

"I'm starting to understand photographers. The camera is stuck to their eyes, blinding them to what's real. Only the naked eye can see what's real. Reality, bam, it hits you in the face. It knocks you down. Wherever you're standing or sitting or hanging out, you take that reality home with you, squinting your eyes, so as not to let it get away. What you saw, what you'll make of it.

"Best I could do, though, is take these pictures. For my backup, you know because I got the reality stored right here in my head. Tell the truth, I didn't mean to take so many, but you know I was being attacked. Attacked by reality, and I couldn't keep it all in my head.

"Look here, Kate. Look at these houses, these used-to-be-houses right down the street from the art museum.

"I started walking down the street, more like I was sailing because my spirit was filled with the ghosts of beautiful places. Then I saw this field, empty like a battlefield after the bodies been hauled off. And I think: What was here? Who did this?

"It's like a foreign place after a war. But I am standing on Woodward Avenue, and if the sun is out, I don't know it because there is nothing but grayness and torn papers and a man carrying a plastic bag walking across a field where nothing is living.

"Down in the distance is the city, big buildings, looking prosperous, but up close...."

"When did you take all these pictures, Suliman?"

"Been taking them."

"You had them developed at a one-hour place."

"Is that the first thing coming to your mind? How much I paid to get my pictures out so fast?"

"I could have taken them to be developed."

"Maybe I didn't want to wait. Maybe I had to keep what was fresh in my mind. But I guess you ain't familiar with the artistic process, the way it feels when something is urgent. Forget the price. It didn't come out of your pocket, so basically it's my business."

He has taken pictures of empty streets, buildings with windows blown out, a street of houses scorched black and boarded up. Abandoned shopping carts on cracked and puddled streets, men waiting at a door. A man is walking his dog through the unchecked growth of weeds. He is smiling, enjoying his cigarette. The police are shaking down three men, their car stopped in the middle of the deserted street. "Rummage," a sign says.

"That's what this is," she says. "This is rummage. Garbage."

She knocks the corkboard to the floor.

He sets the corkboard back against the wall.

"Guess we aren't pretending that the same things matter to us," he says. "Guess you should be going."

# Chapter Thirty-three: Accommodation

Kate sits in her car. She is always driving away: from Casey when he was dying, from a man she wasn't interested in after the first night or the quick afternoon, from Michael, and now from Suliman. He needs to understand deprivation so that she can return.

"Let's face it, girls. We work with the tools we have. It's important to do an inventory of our tools, as well as what our desires are." They laugh. Desire has only one meaning for them. "What you want, what you need," she amends. She is nothing if not careful, handling such dangerous information.

"So what do women want?"

Marriage.

A house. Children.

Charge cards.

Security.

A diamond ring.

Not to work.

"A realistic list," she says. "Anything else?"

A man.

"Isn't that the truth? We can get everything we want if we get the man first. So he moves to the top of the list. A woman without a man is seriously limiting her important choices."

She wonders why no one thinks to contradict her. Haven't their mothers been divorced, short of money, bullied by their husbands, trapped by the long childhoods, the staleness of marriage?

"So we agree that every woman wants a home, children, financial security, and, let's face it, some affection. No, don't smile. Affection is the glue in a marriage, but it isn't the whole picture. Marriage isn't all negligees and moonlight. It's a partnership. With frills.

"All right. You meet the man of your dreams or your daydreams. What's next?"

Getting his attention.

Being sexy.

Looking good.

Playing hard to get.

Pretending he's great.

Giving in.

"What?" she says. "Giving in?"

Like doing what he wants.

Or pretending that you are.

Same thing.

"Accommodation," she says. "It's like wearing gloves. Hiding your hand. Don't forget this. Accommodation is the bottom line. If we learn nothing else from our *mothers—and, of course, we owe them so much for the lessons of life, more than they will ever know—we should learn the lesson of accommodation."*

You use your child. Your job. Your silence. Your compliance. Your body. To keep a man.

The body can fail you. The body does fail you. Kate feels the panic racing. When is the right time for going back?

She has to stay away for a week, long enough to play out the line, but not longer. Things could happen. Another woman in the bed that is hers. The linens and the blankets, hers.

He could call the Dearborn woman. Linda. Talk her back. *I'm sorry, baby. I had me some business. Took off like the careless person I am. Didn't think about what I was doing to you.* She must have been shocked, coming to the motel room, Suliman gone and no way to find him. She must have composed herself so that she could keep the rest of her life together, burying everything about Suliman so that she would not betray herself.

At least, Kate doesn't have to hide it.

# Chapter Thirty-four: Without a Man

It is cold in the house and empty. Michael could be with someone. Why not? She has been a dealer in "someones," pushing the days aside until she has found the next man, less particular with each choice because time is against her.

When she is alone, she does not exist.

When the house warms up, Kate takes a bath. She soaks her hands in detergent and pushes back her cuticles. Her nails are ragged and shapeless. She has let herself go. Roots showing, skin rough, especially at the heels. And gaunt. She laughs. All the years of worrying about gaining weight, and now she wants to take ten pounds, maybe fifteen, and slather them on her hip bones as if they were butter. She needs to fill in the hollows of her cheeks and the bony ridges of her shoulders.

Kate should disappear. But first she should clean out the refrigerator of old salad dressings and cheese as hard as bricks. Empty the spice drawer of oregano and rosemary and sage, so old that they have no aroma. Collect the scraps of paper and the crumpled Kleenex in the wastebaskets, the newspapers and the magazines stacked next to a reading chair, on the end tables, and leave them at the curb in trash bags. Lower the shades, turn down the thermostat to sixty. And drive away. Michael could live there or leave as if a pardon had been ordered: You are free to leave this house where everything was in its place, where every day was the same until it could no longer be endured.

Her mother had packed her suitcases, tucking sachets in the corners so that when she reached the place she had chosen for herself, the fragrance of bay leaves and cinnamon sticks and something else, bitter and pungent, would release itself. The memory of home. She had packed clothes she would wear until she became the person she dreamed for herself, a woman who walked away from an empty house, hours of piled silences, flat words of every day, questions asked, the answers never satisfying, never what she wanted to hear.

She hears the house whisper. Michael has come home. She lets out the water from the tub and towel dries her hair. Tomorrow after school she will get her hair colored. A little lighter this time, the red is too brassy, and her skin looks too pale.

She is not going to pack up her life. She is not going to walk out of the door of her house. She is the preserver of walls and windows, shingles and pavement, the mender and the repairer of damages to carpets and fabrics, to lampshades and tables.

Kate doesn't know exactly when she will go back to the studio, but she will. Suliman will look up from his sketches or from his arranging and rearranging of photographs. "Oh, you back?"

There is nothing else to say.

She will live her life as if nothing was different from yesterday. Because waking up to nothing, going nowhere but to the predictable place of work, is only temporary. She will wait for the right time.

She won't go there in the mornings. She will take more time in dressing. She will read the newspaper while she drinks coffee, real brewed coffee, dripping into the Melitta, a flavored coffee she likes, not the jolting, harsh French roast Suliman bubbles in the old percolator. Some mornings she will condition her hair with a hot oil pack. Use the pumice stone on her feet. Refresh the polish on her nails. People at work have been commenting on her dishevelment. Not that they would call it that. No, it was, "Girl, what is going on with you? Change of life?" "You been sleeping in a homeless shelter, Kate, or what?"

*Casey had asked her, "What would you do, Colleen, if you couldn't make love?"*

*"I wouldn't do anything because I wouldn't exist."*

*Casey laughed a little. "But one day...."*

*"I don't believe in that day."*

She will make it happen, or there is only the walk through scenery, flat and painted.

# Chapter Thirty-five: Lessons

"Girls, after a child is born, it doesn't matter that you got pregnant without... well, without planning to. Decisions were made, and the baby is a fact. You can say that you are too young or that it was a mistake or you have your schooling to finish, but none of that matters to the baby. Everything in its tiny life is up to you.

"Suppose you are hungry? And you can't talk yet. You would cry, too. The baby, let's make her a girl, is sending you a signal. If she could speak, she would say, 'Mom, I would like some food.' It's that simple. Or 'My diaper is wet, and I'm not comfortable.'

"When you are the mother, you have to interpret the signals. Is the baby cold? Uncomfortable? Hungry? Think of the baby as you would think of yourself.

"People say that children don't ask to be born, but that isn't the point. The point is that they are born, and they are somebody's responsibility. Let's say the father isn't interested in the child. It isn't the baby's fault. Someone has got to hold the baby, feed her, clothe her, wash her little body in warm, soapy water. Someone has to talk to her and make her feel loved. Someone has to give her the necessary information for growing up.

"I am talking about words. You don't know them if you don't hear them. When I was pregnant"—the girls look at her in amazement as if the fact of her being a mother has never occurred to them—"I would talk to my baby every day. I would tell her about my day at work just in case she didn't hear it first hand, and what I was seeing as I was driving home. I would discuss the dinner preparations and the snow covering the tree branches. I would talk about my family and my childhood. I would read the newspaper to her. I guess I have myself to blame that she was quite the little chatterbox." The girls laugh at the word, chatterbox.

"There were things I didn't do. I didn't smoke, and I didn't have a drink, not a single one from the moment I knew I was carrying a baby. The aspirin bottle got put in the back of the medicine cabinet. Because we don't know everything, but we do know how slender the barrier is between mother and unborn child. You eat some pizza and get indigestion. So does your daughter, the little girl who isn't born yet. If you get drunk, she does, too. If you are upset, so is your unborn child.

"All we can do is think about that child as part of ourselves. Because that's the reality of it. All we can do is try to make the world, inside and outside, as good as we possibly can."

In her Life Skills class the lessons are the same as when the girls were the children of immigrants, and their dreams were easy to define: a house in a nice neighborhood, a garden, family dinners, new clothes for Easter.

"How come you always talking like everyone going to get married?"

"Most people do marry, I believe."

"I guess you ain't been looking around."

She doesn't know the girl's name, Natasha or LaKeshia. She hasn't learned their names this semester, and now this Keisha or LaTasha is changing the rules. And why not? There is nothing to lose.

"Now that you mention it, women are more on their own."

"Have been, you ask me. Who in here got babies, huh?" She is asking a question that doesn't fit with the lesson plan or the expectations or the dream.

"Me, I got a little girl, probably be in school before I get out."

Kate has been talking to the ghosts of girls who had worn dresses to school, who had gone home to do schoolwork and helped their mothers with dinner. She has been decorating uninhabited houses and preparing menus for phantom meals. She has been fabricating the waking up of a household, the last minutes in the warm bed, the breakfast, and the school bus.

"We should talk about children," she says. "The bringing up of children."

It isn't in the plan, not anyone's plan. She has wandered into a dangerous area.

"In the abstract," she says, "the way it should be."

The girls turn away. They are turning away from her. She has nothing to tell them but of things that will never be. She has never been talking to them.

She says to the sullen girls, "Let's spend this time talking about mothering."

She doesn't know when a girl is pregnant because she has stopped noticing. She is always surprised when she gets the note from the counselor about the prolonged absence, the inevitable pregnancy. But Shannon was not in her plans either, not in the way Michael accused her, shouting, "Aren't there enough links in this chain?"

"Having a child is the choice that has been made," she says, careful of her language, afraid of the times that are chaotic but not free. "Now the choice is to decide the real meaning of the word, mother. That will be your name. You will be their only mother."

"What if it ain't your choice, not one bit of it?"

She has to be careful. This is no time for trouble at school. "Well, there are people who can help."

The girls laugh. It is a mirthless laugh.

"Your own mother, for example."

"I got two babies," Keisha says. She is Kate's attendance clerk, sixteen or seventeen. Kate has never thought to ask her, "How old are you? Where do you live? What is on the other side of the door you open after school?" And now, the questions that have to be asked are too dangerous for Kate: "Who is the father? Who takes care of your baby? How do you feel about being a mother?"

"First time, I didn't even know I was pregnant," Keisha says. "Like my body wasn't ever something I noticed. I was just me. And then there was the baby, and I was thinking, 'What does this baby have to do with me? How come I got this baby?' And my mama was so mad, but then she cried. She kept saying that it was never going to stop, that it was unfair. 'Snatching away her baby's innocence,' that's what she said."

"What I got to ask is why babies are the punishment," another girl says. "You know, for five minutes of letting someone talk nice to you. For thinking, what's the big deal anyhow?"

"My mama's boyfriend beat me up good when I turned up pregnant. Like who do he think he is? He got kids in practically every house on the street."

"Bet he don't support none of them either." There is laughter.

"I had to move out the house. My daddy said he wasn't living with a whore. I wrote it down later, 'h-o-r-e.' I didn't even know about the 'w.'"

"Neither did your daddy." More laughter.

"What we need is a baby-raising class, not a how-to-set-up-a-perfect-household. No insult intended, Mrs. Connally."

"How about we learn some baby-prevention?"

"Girl, that too simple. Stay at home. By yourself."

"All right, girls, all right. This is something for me to think about. For all of us to think about. Thank you for your candor. Your honesty, I mean."

"I should retire," she says to the business math teacher.

"You got to be crazy! And exactly what you going to do with the time? I'm telling you, in August I am like to go crazy with boredom. All I got to look forward to is the opening meeting and the people I couldn't wait to see the backs of a few months ago."

"I have enough years."

"That's the last thing it's about. Remember the art teacher? Going to be a painter. All day and all night, that's what he was going do: paint, paint, paint. It must have scared him to death because we went to his funeral not three months after the retirement luncheon."

"Year after year, I just can't...."

"You thinking too far ahead. Come on out with us after school. Been a long time since you did a Friday afternoon at Aladdin's. It's always something."

Kate laughs. "You mean it's always someone."

"That, too. For sure."

# Chapter Thirty-six: Old Times

She goes to Aladdin's. Stephon is there sitting in a booth by himself. It is Friday, teacher's day, but he is the only one from school.

"You been keeping yourself scarce," he says when she sits down across from him.

"You 'cut me loose,' remember?"

"Now, Kate, that woman was nothing but a little diversion."

"It looked serious to me."

"Well, actually, it lasted a while. I thought I was in love."

"I'm glad, Stephon."

"I'm not so glad. That woman didn't want the white-collar teacher life. She said. 'I can't make it on nickels and dimes.' I sure tried to talk her out of leaving. I'll tell you the truth, Kate. I talked so fast that I didn't know what was true and what was my story-telling ability. But talk is talk, and she wanted stuff. A fancy car, and I can't even make my car payments most months."

"I remember that."

"I'm not hitting you up, Kate."

"It wouldn't do you any good, Stephon."

"You taking care of someone?"

"Something like that. I should know better."

"Someone has to be the giver, and someone has to be the taker. It's the rule of life. Only thing is, women have a hard time with that. A woman isn't happy when a man is in the taking position. She starts wondering what's she doing with him in the first place.

"Trouble with both of us is not looking ahead and seeing the realities. Speaking of which, you are looking quite sexy these days. Very delectable."

"I look terrible."

"Now let me be the judge. You got your juices flowing. Wherever you been, it's been good for you. Speaking of which...."

"I can't afford it, Stephon."

"No charge."

"That's not what I can't afford."

"I can't believe I'm hearing this from you, Kate. Aren't you always looking for a good time? That's what you told me. Two people are sitting here wasting time in Aladdin's. Come on, girl. Let's take advantage of the time."

The telephone is ringing, and she think-dreams that it is Suliman calling her, asking her to come back. She is happy; she will go back. But then there is a voice, a man whispering, "Uh-uhn, honey, I'm here by myself."

She is in Stephon's bed, and it is after two o'clock in the morning. She thinks of Michael, sleepless in the dark house and hating her.

"You could have wakened me, Stephon."

"Kate, how long have I known you? Don't even answer. We both know. I got to ask you what you are running home to. Mr. Connally does not care if you ever come home. Now, if there is some place else you have to be, fine. I can understand that, but not this Cinderella business."

"These are rules I make for myself, Stephon."

"But you got a new man, right? The one who is taking too much."

She can't answer Stephon. There is humiliation and there is anger and there is missing Suliman.

"A woman thinks that if a man cares about her, he'll prove it with money. Stuff, necessary or not. I sure would like to know who made those payment plans. But sometimes the tables get turned. I'm not talking about me. I should have been more of a gentleman because you are good people. You got a big heart, but you never got used to it."

"I don't like being exploited."

"That's what you call it. Maybe you are being needed. What does this guy do?"

"He's an artist."

"Say no more. A con artist."

"No. He is an innocent person."

"That's not all bad."

"I'm going home, Stephon. You have your business to take care of, and I need my beauty sleep."

"You'd be beautiful any time, Kate."

"I'm old."

"White women shouldn't have learned to count. You done forgot the big picture, girl. It's just life, Kate, something we have to accept in spite of everything."

Kate wants to cry and let Stephon hold her in his arms. But Stephon will close himself like a book. He has just so much kindness in him; there is mostly impatience.

"You would be one lucky woman if your house burned down."

"Thanks, Stephon."

"I'm talking about freedom, Kate."

# Chapter Thirty-seven: Reconciliation

An entire street has disappeared. Kate wants to stop the car and ask a passer-by: What happened to Evaline Street? She has made the wrong turn, that's all. On this bright morning that she is going back to Suliman.
*He will say, "What took you so long?"*
*"I was waiting until you got hungry enough."*
*"Food ain't the problem. There are other necessities. Ever occur to you that I like having you around?"*
*"No, it never occurred to me."*
*"I just need you, okay."*
*"I don't care what your reason is,"* she will say. *"I can't live without the smell of paint."*

She will tell Suliman that in the endless week of separation she has felt herself grow faint like the spirits in the underworld who fade away when there is no offering of blood or prayers of remembrance. Like Casey's shadow because she had set nothing on the altar of memory.

There is a car parked near the door of the studio. If it is new, it is the Dearborn woman. Of course, the woman would take him back. Her days must have been as uneventful as the flipped pages of a 365-day-calendar, nothing different except for the numbers.

The car isn't new. The side view mirror hangs down like a broken branch, there is a patch of rust on the trunk, a passenger side window that isn't quite shut. The car could belong to some lean girl with caramel skin and smoky eyes. Kate hasn't got the energy for anything but the reunion that she has imagined. She will come back another day when she will not be frightened by an old car.

Her fingers wander again to the lump under her hair, behind her ear. It has always been there, hasn't it? The sliding of her fingers to the spot feels so familiar; the lump, no, not a lump, more like a hive or a bite. It has always been there, she is sure.

She knows better. She knows exactly when she felt it for the first time, during the first month when they were packing to leave the old studio. If it had been different between them, she would have said to Suliman, "Feel this bump. What do you think it is?" But it has always been her conviction that a young man approaches an older woman as he would a plunge into icy water. The water is an unpleasant shock, and then it will become acceptable, almost enjoyable. It will never be what he wants. The little irregularities are kept private. And she had been too busy for her hand to drift beneath the hair and acknowledge the presence of the lump.

In the beauty salon indifferent fingers find it, stop, move away and return. "You know, there is something here," the shampoo girl says. "Do you know?"

She says she knows. It's nothing. Been there forever. After all, it is not the obligation of a shampoo girl to share in the alarm.

"A clogged oil gland, that's all."

It will have to be taken care of even though she needs all the energy she can muster for going back to Suliman.

She goes to Michael's room at night. He is sleeping. She sits on the edge of the bed and listens to his breathing. Such a narrow bed, like a monk's. The curtains, the posters, the prints, the clutter of girl things have been packed away. Of course, he wouldn't want to live in a room that reminded him of Shannon and how she left. The austerity made it his own. An unfinished chest of drawers, a shoe rack in the closet, and wooden hangers for his suits. How they had argued about hangers until she had brought out a summer suit with ridges that couldn't be steamed out except at the cleaner's.

"Kate?" he says. He was always quick to wake up as if he hadn't really been sleeping, just waiting. "What's wrong?" As if all the silent years had not been crouching behind the closed doors, the unsaid words gathering and straining against the months and the years.

"I think...." She begins to cry.

"Whatever it is, I'll take care of it." He is sitting up now, looking at her, not touching her, but looking at her.

"I have a lump." She draws his fingers to the spot.

"Oh, yes. A cyst. It could be nothing."

"It is always something, Michael."

"We can take care of it."

He sits in her room all night. She would like him to lie down beside her as if all past time had been a dream or a mistake.

# Chapter Thirty-eight: Family Matters

They have agreed not to tell Shannon until there has been a firm diagnosis.

But the decision has been made. There are streets that have vanished from the map of Kate's travels. The studio and Evaline Street have been swallowed up as if they had never existed.

She lifts her hair and lets it fall over the paper gown while she is waiting for the otolaryngologist. Her hair. It will have to go.

"You have given this good time for growing, Mrs. Connally," the otolaryngologist says. She never says his name, Sink or Sing, she doesn't want to make a mistake. "No doubt you thought it was nothing." He wasn't going to excuse her for the months of denial. She had imagined some days that it was smaller, no bigger than a pea, living under the surface of skin, shrinking and growing.

"'Nothing' often requires some attention," the otolaryngologist says, a favorite axiom of his. She can tell by the way he smiles when he says it. "This little nothing is the size of a lima bean. I will excise it. There is nothing else to do."

"You mean surgery? I don't have time for surgery right now. I am a teacher, and there is...."

She wants to chart for the otolaryngologist the impossibilities of finding even a half a day for outpatient surgery.

"Look where it is located," he says, drawing a triangle with his pencil. Whish, whish, whish. He does not touch her skin. "Many functions in this little space. The trigeminal nerve." He says more to himself than to her, "The miracle of it, the wonder."

"Don't you have some kind of x-ray machine to take a look? To be sure that it is something."

"Oh, it is something, no matter what it is. Something that must not be where it is any more.

"Some will tell you, needle biopsy, but the danger if this is malignant, the cells released...." He closes his eyes, and she imagines for him the scurrying of cells, celebrating their freedom.

"We will play it safe."

"Can we wait? Until school is over in a few months?"

His fingers play over the hard surface, like a diviner, anticipating water. "Waiting is always a possibility."

Michael rises when she comes into the waiting room. There was the time, when... but here he is, jumping to his feet when she comes out of the examining room.

"We are supposed to watch it for a while."

"That's all? Let me talk to him."

"No, not all. A surgery...here...when school is out."
"That's months away."
"It is contained." Whatever "it" is.

# Chapter Thirty-nine: The Magic of Two

"Girls, at the end of the line, or even at the beginning of the line, there are going to be problems. You don't want to be standing there alone, believe me. You want a husband, children—well, ones that have grown up. The little ones, you don't want to make a hard life for the little ones. If you can help it.

"People want to believe that bad things only happen to someone else. For instance, you read in the newspaper that a house has burned down. Everything is lost, and the husband and wife are standing in the ashes of everything that can never be replaced: the old couch, the kitchen table, the towels, the favorite pair of shoes. Gone, no matter how thoroughly they sift through the debris.

"You never think it would be you. No. It is beyond your imaginations, walking up to the house, and the bricks are charred, the windows broken, the floor is smoking, the roof is a tangle of burnt beams. These disasters are not in your plans.

"Sometimes on television after a tornado, somewhere else, of course, or it could have been a hurricane, a woman is standing in front of the place where her little frame house once stood. Or her trailer. She doesn't know how to get back to the time before the storm, to restore the rickety table, the tattered armchair, the refrigerator that makes too much noise and seems to wiggle across the floor when she isn't looking. We feel sad for the woman. Where is her husband? What about her children? We will not be comforted until someone rescues her. A son or the husband who has been at the police station reclaiming some of the documents rescued from the wreckage. Then we can accept the shock of disaster. The family absorbs it."

Every day she thinks about going to the studio. For an hour to talk. Yes, she was angry that day, she meant to come back, but now there is something that has to be handled at home. And how to say that she has regained home and husband for the very reasons they have existed. She would have to say, "I need my husband for this...situation, a family situation."

It is better not to go to Suliman. There is the risk. Even if she takes half a day from school, Michael will know. They are Siamese twins; they couldn't separate now if they wanted to. And they had wanted that once, but not now.

Suliman recedes. She will never go back to him. She will never try.

There are so many appointments, but Michael drives her to the oncologist, the radiologist, the labs. She won't ask him how long it has been since he has worked, probably at some public relations firm with long hours and a salary that never stretched far enough.

"You should retire," he says. They are driving to the oncologist, one last decision to make, chemo or surgery. Or both.

"I'm thinking about using my sick days."

"Can't you cash them in? We could use the money."

We. She should open the door of the car and step out into traffic. Cars will swerve away, but someone will not be able to respond in time.

"That's something to think about," she says.

"Girls, what's the most important element in a marriage?" There is no snickering. This is a serious question.

"Love." *Of course, love.*

"Security. Children."

"A house."

*No one mentions sex. It is wrapped up somewhere in the balloon word, love, crowded by so many other inadequate words, waterlogged with disappointment.*

"Someone is always there for you."

*She nods at the girl, the bright-haired, peach-skinned girl, the one who is always being stopped in the hall, turning her pale eyes to some tall, still-not-manly boy, but there is the promise. The girl is speculating that this one could be The One. Or maybe not.*

"Yes. That's the beauty of marriage. Fidelity. Should I spell that word?" *She is conjuring up the mirage of two. The husband and wife late at night, heads bent over the bills. How will they manage? They will do it somehow because they are partners. The hand on a forehead. Dear, you will feel better soon. An accident, a car, perhaps a knife cut that is bleeding too profusely for home first aid.* "The husband is there. You, the wife, are there. Nothing is unbearable when the number is two."

"Two," she says. "The magic number is two." *Kate writes it on the board. The girls must know how important it is. Kate walks across the room to the single green board with the yellow stick of chalk is in her hand.* "The magic number is two."

# Chapter Forty: Crowning Glory

She has her hair cut. The hairdresser pulls it smooth so that it falls easily beneath the line of her jaw. He says that the new style becomes her.

She is preparing herself for losses. If she approaches them gradually, perhaps they will not be so painful. The diminished energy, the growing pallor, skin like fraying fabric, the hair thinning, separating, caught in the brush, washed away in the shower.

"Girls, your hair is your crowning glory. Sometimes I wonder if you understand that. What is so glorious and beautiful should not be tampered with. I am talking about your natural hair color. It is going to last just so long, the original, made-for-you lovely hair. It shouldn't be bleached or tangled or covered with flat, unnatural colors. Certainly it should not be ironed or permed to death.

"How many of you wash your hair every day?"

There are hands; the girls want her approval in spite of the crimes they have been committing against their hair.

"Experts warn against too frequent washing because the natural oils go down the drain with the rinse water. For instance, American women could never sell their hair."

The girls look at her in amazement at the idea of selling hair.

"Yes, it's true, beautiful, luxurious hair can be sold, but it comes from countries where women rarely wash their hair."

The girls grimace with distaste.

"They might oil it and, on the occasions of washing, dry it in the hot sun." They share the vision of black, black hair spread out on fingers and falling on shoulders, the sun touching it like a blessing.

"This hair has been treasured. For these women, it is like money in the bank.

"No, we aren't going into the hair-selling business." The girls laugh. She has gotten their attention. "However, we should think about the mortality of our hair. Yes, hair dies. I don't mean dyes as in color. What remains is gray, the absence of color."

The girls look at her in disbelief. They will resemble their mothers, their grandmothers, old women.

"Your skin, your hair, your eyebrows, your lashes, they lose the color that is uniquely yours. The beauty you have been handed like a gift. Don't laugh. To be young is to be beautiful. That's why we say that youth is wasted on the young. You are so busy being self-conscious that you are missing the miracle of your beauty."

She is embarrassed. It is not like her to become so personal.

"We are going to think about taking better care of our hair. We are going to be more gentle with that crowning glory. Let's stop twisting and burning and piling on all that goop. Be sure to cut off those brittle ends every few months. And keep your head off the ironing board. A dress wears out from too much washing and ironing. What do you think will happen to your hair?"

*The girls look contrite. They regret the curling irons and hot curlers. They hear the sizzle of hair burning as they pull it and wind it over the hot tongs. As they aim their dryers at the lifted hair.*

"So what is a good method of hair care? Stacy, what do you do, for instance?" She knows that Stacy will be willing to talk about the honey, straight hair that she flings from side to side as she walks down the hall and when she settles into her seat in class.

"Well, Mrs. Connally, I do wash my hair every day, but I never use a dryer. I use baby shampoo because my mom says it isn't too harsh. And a little bit of conditioner."

"Boys use soap," another girl says. "Like my brother. Why don't boys care?"

"That's another story," Kate says. "We have our problems. They have theirs."

*They have made a list. Do not wash your hair more than four times a week. Get a good hair cut so that you don't have to use rollers or curling irons. Do not press your hair with an iron. If you want to be blonde, keep away from harsh peroxides. But why would you want to be blonde? Conditioning does not mean going to the gym. It means adding some moisture to your hair. Use a brush with soft bristles. Wear a hat in the sun if you are out all day.*

"What about you, Mrs. Connally? Is that your original hair color?"

"As close as I am going to get it," she says, "because I think that nature can be cruel to women in some ways. We can help nature along but only when we have to."

Her hair must be completely gray by now. So much else has gone that the strawberry gold of her hair could not have survived the years.

# Chapter Forty-one: A New Schedule

The principal stands up and shakes Michael's hand. They talk as if Kate is not capable of planning the end of her career: the sudden turn of a life veering away from bells and room changes, lunch duty, and after-school meetings on Wednesday.

"She could use her days," the principal says, turning the pages in Kate's employment record. "Or take a medical without pay." He hesitates. "She could retire. There are certainly enough years. But then the life insurance policy is void, once she retires. The $25,000."

What is Michael's bet on survival?

He has calculated the dollars, speculating on what is possible. He is not a dreamer.

But he is quick with numbers. Fifty percent of the pension for the surviving spouse if you are planning on a long life doesn't do it. The twenty-five thousand can be gone in a year. And she probably won't die from the lymphoma. She will not be a teacher who makes $70,000, but half of that sum will work until it is time for social security for both of them. That's the plan. It is in both of their heads, so she doesn't need to speak. He is her husband; he can speak for her. Because one plus one equal two, and two are one.

"She should retire," Michael says. "It is the best solution."

The principal says that Kate will be missed. He wants to know if she will finish out the semester or take her sick days until the retirement process is completed.

"I'm working," she says, "until the surgery. About a month." She hears Michael's silent concurrence.

She should call Suliman. "How are you doing? Miss you, but then this happened. And 'this' turned into something I hadn't counted on. My husband and I...." And he will say, "Good, that's good, Kate. I mean I don't like the way things are going without you, but it's good for you."

But she doesn't call. She has an image to preserve.

## Chapter Forty-two: Reductions

"It won't end with the surgery," Michael tells Shannon on the phone. "I'll need you. Well, your mother will need you."

Kate isn't included in this discussion of her body. It is her cancer, her surgery, her chemo. It makes her angry that they have finally found a way to unman her, father and daughter, whose only weapons had been flight. Now in her helplessness, she has become a woman, powerless and dependent. Now Shannon will come home.

## Chapter Forty-three: The Poisoned Body

"Girls, the key to securing your home against invasion is vigilance. Carelessness is your enemy. Remember this when you leave the groceries on the kitchen counter or forget to refrigerate the milk. When you don't remove that blue cotton sock from the load of whites. All the bleach in the world will never make those whites the same. There will be a haunting of blue forever. Carelessness cannot be undone. It brings waste and disease and despair.

"Yes, despair. Tasks mount up when they are not tended to. Dust on the blinds, towels crumpled up in the linen closet, cutlery dumped in a drawer, the pots and skillets hopelessly jumbled under the sink, the confusion of cans and boxes shoved into the food pantry.

"Girls, think about those survivors of an earthquake or a flood. A man or a woman turns to the television camera, says words that cannot be equal to the despair they feel. The hopelessness. How can my life ever return to the way it was? The woman picks up a picture frame or a toy that is miraculously intact. What can be done with it? Where is the beginning of order and re-order?"

The girls look stunned and bereft as if their own possessions, present and future, have been caught up in a maelstrom.

"Diligence," she repeats. "It is not so easy as you think. It is not only watching; it is being armed."

The surgeon tells her that she doesn't have to be kept overnight.

"But someone will have to be here at all times," the surgeon says. "During the procedure."

"Yes," she says. "My husband."

It is a brief surgery. The lump is excised, and then there is the aching that never quite goes away even though Michael is quick to bring the pain pills right on the minute every four hours. "But sooner if you need them, Kate."

Each procedure puts her outside of the life of the house. She is ushered out of her room and back again like a guest. She cannot manage the new terrain herself: the biopsies, the bone marrow test, the pain sending her reeling into a speechless place, the hollowed-out day for chemo, days outside time. Because time is meant to measure ordinary things like making the bed and going to the supermarket, checking the time for a movie, and grating the cheese for pizza. Time is suspended for the impossible and the unthinkable, like war and childbirth and a scalpel parting the skin. The drip of the IV, the colorless liquid, so ominous in its pallor.

"I can handle all of this," she says to Shannon, who helps her to the bathroom, but Shannon doesn't hear her. Or she hasn't spoken.

"Don't look in the mirror, Mom." But Kate does and she laughs. "Dad has called someone. About a wig," Shannon says.

The kitchen sounds comfort her. The lid set on a pot, the knives, forks, and spoons tumbled into the dishwasher, the sliding of the broom across the floor. She conjures for herself the ladles and the stirring spoons, the spatulas and the whisks set out on the counter like flowers in a vase; the good dishes set above the every day dishes, a cup and a saucer set out for decoration on the upper shelves. She counts from memory the linen napkins and the cotton and polyester blend on the pantry shelf, each one creased with equal care. She conjures up the mangled napkin ring that fell into the disposal, which she could not bring herself to throw it out.

Shannon spoons applesauce and soft egg into her mouth. "Is this revenge?" she asks. But Shannon smiles as if she has not heard, the spoon persistent against her pressed lips, the clenched teeth.

Kate has lost her voice.

In the silence she can stack one loss upon another as if she were arranging canned goods in a pantry.

Casey.

Shannon.

Michael.

The strawberry blonde of her hair.

The young man, his name lost for a moment, and the street name as well. She can almost remember it. He took up so much energy. The money and her car weren't going to hold out much longer the way she was piling up the miles. To drive to Hamtramck. It makes her laugh. What was she thinking? And the gas, what with prices soaring.

And he wanted a car or the only car. Suliman. The one who took too much.

The hand mirrors and the mirror standing like an easel in the upstairs hallway are removed. She isn't supposed to see who she has become.

Every object is a mirror: the window at night, the back of a spoon, the gloss of a lamp base or the shine of a plate. She doesn't need them. She contemplates her naked self; she is her own mirror. The stripped-down model, my new look, she says, but all the saying is in her head. Hairless, bloodless, skin stretched over bone. Who knew that bones could be so beautiful?

*She would tell the girls: "The body can betray you. Either way, too fat or too thin, the body is going to betray you. And fail you. But in the mirror of your imagining, you are still yourself, the self you have been creating from the first moment you understand it is your most important creation."*

# Chapter Forty-four: The New Body

"I can take a shower myself," she says to Shannon, not unkindly because her daughter has done her duty. Kate has not expected that. But she tells her that Michael can do the shopping and prepare the meals. The home aides come every day.

"Your dad and I can manage, not that we won't miss you...."

"Are you sure, Mom?"

"I'm so much better."

Kate is moving into her new body. She hasn't considered the possibility of dying. She has paid enough; she doesn't have to die. Her new self is gaunt, rubbed raw, burnt. The dull ache whose source she can't locate is everywhere.

She stays in her bedroom, wearing floppy robes and soft slippers because the hard surfaces of clothing hurt her bones and move too harshly against her skin. She would prefer to be wrapped loosely in silk.

The robes aren't silk; they are cotton and easy to wash. There is the smell of illness. She doesn't notice it, but the home aides do. Their faces stiffen a little, right before they smile with their false brightness. Going to be a good day today, whisking away the soiled robe, the suspicious sheets. The mornings are long half-dreams. Kate doesn't mind because it is her only privacy. During her public hours there is Michael and the visiting nurse. The aide feeds her and bathes her, strips away the soiled linens while Kate turns away in embarrassment at what has leaked from her poisoned body.

She is a poisoned body, where the rowdy, raucous cells run riot as if there were a party going on. Then the rescuers come, their lances dripping good poison.

Of course, rescue is better than the alternative, or it would be called something else—like appropriation. Her life, her body, her every movement are the responsibilities of other people. She must be done to. She is a stranger to the person she has become.

She is not the self from before, the one with red hair and smooth legs, the seductive kindnesses that were her tools. If she were her old self, she would tell Michael that he is the head nurse when he comes marching into her room, plumps up her pillows, raises the windows—it must be the smell of the enemy cells that has become so natural to her—and asks: "Strong enough today for an outing?" Where does he want her to go? She isn't asking yet. She is staying where she is.

# Chapter Forty-five: The Right Time

*"Timing is everything, girls. Who said that?"*

*"Someone like Shakespeare."*

*"The President."*

*"It's true for everyone, no matter who said it, but it had to be someone in charge of making things come out right. Five extra minutes in the oven, and you have a dried-out cake or baked chicken that is going to taste like cardboard. And we all know what damage an extra minute in the microwave can do. The clock is the master in everything. For instance, nail polish must be completely dry, so it won't stick to the inside of your gloves. Worst-case scenario, girls. Putting on your gloves when your nail polish hasn't had time to dry.*

*"You have to know when it is time to leave. It's simple if you pay attention. Let's say that your hostess sneaks a glance at the clock or looks at the imaginary watch on her wrist. Knowing that it's time to leave is about as important as showing up on time, but it is trickier."*

*"How can you be sure that it's time to leave?" The girls find the problem of knowing when to leave more compelling than the exactitude demanded by cooking.*

*"Every situation has its own rules. Be on your toes. Pay attention. Watch for the right time, and you will never have to experience the wrong time."*

# Chapter Forty-six: Remembering Suliman

*She is lying with her back to Suliman. His hand is on her hip. It is evening and the only light comes from street through the high windows. There are candles, but she doesn't light them now that he is painting.*

"Fire," she says, "everything will be lost. All that I have worked for."

"There are two of us," he says, "two of us working."

"You will be the one they talk about. People will drink wine out of plastic cups and stand in front of your paintings. They will shake your hand. Praise your work. And where will I be? Taking down addresses. Filling the wine glasses for the people who are coming in the door."

"I bet you won't be buying expensive wine. Probably the kind with screw-off tops."

"Someone might steal the corkscrew."

There are two of them dreaming in this bed.

"I am going to build a loft," he says, "so that we can have a separate place from the studio. For resting, you know."

"It's a waste of time. Building a loft. We don't need it."

He laughs because he is overcome and does not want to cry. "I can't believe that this is mine. A good life used to be a cell and a bed and maybe people leaving me alone. A big deal was getting a book or a sketchpad."

"I can't bear to think of you in that place."

He says that it wasn't horrible. "It was like high school. You have to be in a certain place at a certain time. No decisions have to be made. Where to go. What to do. Prison was safety, not like Ellis Island where you were always in danger of making the wrong choice."

Ellis Island was wasted on him. Sure, he regretted the day he walked away, but it was the only choice he knew how to make.

Prison was a map. And he was good at reading maps, at sensing which corner to turn, which place to avoid.

"It was my place of growing up. Isn't that what choosing means? You are growing up."

"I don't believe in choosing," she says. "I believe in the moment arriving."

"That is too much philosophy."

"Living is a matter of accommodating," she says.

"Too heavy," he says. "Besides, defeat is not what I am about."

He took up with the Muslims in prison. The Muslim brothers had claimed some shares of his soul and a big chunk of his commitment, but he got the bigger share, safety. They called him brother and they gave him a name that had dignity, Brother Suliman. Dignity is the essence of a man. The Muslims liked the idea of essences, smoky and elusive, slipping under doors and into the cells.

"God is an essence, brother. Do you feel the spirit of God in this room?" He was glad they didn't call God by the name of Allah. He was still his old self about things like that.

*His old self had been a boy strutting around so that he didn't have to crawl. His old self was a thug because he didn't know what to do about the awe he felt when he saw the morning light streaming through a window. The sight was beautiful to him, but he didn't know what to do with it.*

*Prison gave him time to think. All the empty days and nights had given him a lesson in time—as if someone had said to him: You have the luxury of empty time, but you have to pay it back.*

*Freedom in reverse. When he understood that, he stopped regretting the day he walked away from Ellis Island. He wasn't ready to be the someone that they wanted to redeem. He wasn't the kind to be a good citizen. He doesn't know too many artists who are good citizens.*

*"You mean like paying taxes," she says.*

*"Only when you got a job," he says.*

# Chapter Forty-seven: Returning to Life

"Girls," she says, and the faces are black or dusky or brown. "Girls, life doesn't always give you little boxes with diamond rings in them. If that's what you expect, then you will be very disappointed. Disappointment is what you have to be prepared for."

"You tell it," someone says, and the girls are only sixteen or seventeen. They know too much already.

"So what do you do? You get tough, but not so that anyone notices. It all has to be on the inside. The wariness. To be wary is to be careful. A spy would be wary, always watching. A soldier would be wary in enemy territory. You are always in enemy territory, and if you turn out to be wrong, well, you have been careful, haven't you? So nothing has been lost."

"So how come we always losing?"

"You give too much."

"Ain't we suppose to give?"

"That's what I learned at church."

"You give what you can afford to. Money in the box when it is passed. A favor to a friend. Helping an old person with heavy packages. Listening to your friends when they are in trouble. But don't give if what you expect in return is your heart's desire. You won't get what you want, not if you piled all your worldly goods on the bonfire of your intentions and your longings. The only thing that will happen is that they will no longer be yours and they will be of no value to anyone.

"You don't say, 'I will do anything for you,' or 'I love you more than anything.' No, not even to your child. Because you have to leave something for yourself so that you can continue living when the man leaves or turns away in his heart from you. When the child grows up and goes his own way.

"You can't stop other people's lives from happening the way they want it. But you can't let their toughness get in the way of your toughness, which is the only way you are going to get what belongs to you."

"What belongs to us?"

"Your body, the complication of feelings that we call our selves. Protect it with some kind of armor. Or wrap your arms around yourself if that is the best you can do. Plant your feet and say, 'No, I don't have that to give. I only have this much to spare.'

"It isn't selfishness. I know what we have all been taught, but protection is more important." Someone laughs, and she says, "Oh yes, that kind of protection, too. There are other kinds. That's all I'm saying. For instance, think of turtles or snails."

She wonders if the girls have ever seen the shell of a snail. Turtles then. The giant creatures at the zoo who lie as still as boulders.

"Would a turtle dream of crawling out of the shell built to protect him from just about everything a turtle could imagine happening to him?"

"Then how he get caught?"

"He couldn't imagine the human part. But from all other things, his shell protects him. Let's say he comes out for a look around. He is all softness, naked like a baby."

"Better hurry back inside, Mr. Turtle."

"Hawk gonna get you."

"You said it, girls. Think of yourself as turtles. They have fun, too. Although I am having a hard time imagining exactly how."

"Never saw no turtle...."

"Protection. A woman must provide her own protection. That's all I am saying."

"We should get a walker," Michael says, "just for balance."

Kate prefers to guide herself from bedroom to bathroom, down the stairs and to the kitchen, with the flat of her hand on a wall, a chest of drawers, a chair. She hasn't been left with much. But she has her toughness.

Toughness is what has gotten her through the radiation and the chemotherapy. She didn't cry when her hair fell out. She laughed and said that she would have considered baldness a long time ago if she had known that her head was shaped so perfectly.

Toughness gets you to where you want to be. Of course, she would want to use a different word for it. A word carries its positives and its negatives. She would want to choose the right word for exactly who she has become.

Now she must protect herself from the memory of who she was. She has been purged of that woman. The poison has raced like rats in the corridors of her blood stream, peering around a corner, seeing what is being attacked, what to save for later.

She has been illuminated, penetrated, burnt, and emptied.

# Chapter Forty-eight: Reports of Suliman

Kate lets the rusty gray hair have its way. She is amused and horrified, but she won't cover the stubble of new hair.

Even if Suliman would come. He would ask her why she didn't tell him, and she would answer that there wasn't time. But that wouldn't be the truth. She was trading: Michael for Suliman, husband for lover, because the husband and wife have a contract. Kate and Suliman have not signed their names to any contract. Only Kate's name appeared on the lease, the phone bill, the gas, the electricity.

Who was paying those bills? There would be shut-off notices, an interruption of services.

"Your young man has been calling," Michael says. "Suliman. He wanted to speak to you."

"Did you tell him?"

"Eventually. I had to pry out of him who he was. He said you were his patron. But I got the picture."

"What did he want?"

"To tell you about his paintings. 'I don't want her being disappointed in me even though our business be over,' he said. 'What business?' I asked. 'Art business and some personal business.' I told him that I was more aware of the personal business than he might think. He didn't hesitate. No wavering or the click of a line going dead. On the contrary, he said, 'You left some territory open, and nature got to fill those empty places. Can't be blaming anyone when we all got a part in what was happening.'"

"I don't want to hear about this, Michael."

"Suliman wants to pay his debt. He said that he owes you everything, that he has been painting as if there were demons inside of him. 'Good demons,' he said. He wanted you to know that."

"That's good."

"And he wants to see you. 'Least I can do for the woman who saw the light in me and didn't stop giving.' Apparently you complained a lot about the giving part, according to Suliman."

"You learned all of this in one conversation?"

"Oh no. I have been going to the studio. I am very impressed with your young man, but he isn't one for practical details. So I have stepped in—with a little advice, some ideas...."

"And money."

"It's a family investment. He has talent and—I don't need to tell you—charisma. He has got to lose the rapper look. Nothing more than a change of wardrobe, white shirt, khakis, loafers, a sports coat. His paintings can be the street, but he has to be above it."

"Now Suliman is your project."

"I am picking up where you left off."

"I won't see him."
"I told him that."
"He must have been relieved."
"He wanted to show you his work. But he understood."

# Chapter Forty-nine: Dream Speak

Michael says, or he would have said if they spoke honestly with each other, "I won't lie to you, Kate. I see your Suliman quite a bit. At first, I was curious about what sent you off so early in the morning and what kept you so late at night. I didn't want to notice, but the evidence couldn't be avoided. I jolted awake when you did. I followed you in all your movements as if there were no walls between us. You set out your underwear on the turned-back cover. You hung your dress on the door of the closet and placed your shoes near the door. I dozed off while you showered, but I was awake when you put up your wet hair and gave that final scrubbing to your skin with the loofah. To wake up the skin, you would have told me. If we were speaking in words.

"I anticipated the slide of your stocking feet through the house to the kitchen. One of your rules: no outdoor shoes in the house.

"The whole time, Kate, we were speaking to each other in the way of people who know each other through love and hate. Think of the intimacy we have shared, the complexity of it. The love…so brief. The longer stint of hate. And this. I would call it symbiotic. Living together even though I suspect that the meaning, living on each other, would be more accurate.

"I'm not unhappy with the way things are. Are you? I don't think so. You are so serene. At first, I have to admit, I wanted you defeated, but your own body has done that for me. The body has its dictates, no matter what household remedies you might employ. Isn't that so?

"Then I wanted to know him. I went to the studio. It was your handiwork, I could see that. Two elements were working at once. The simplicity of the whiteness, all the complexity belonging to the work. I saw the racks where the painting surfaces were arranged by size and by material. 'Whose order is imposed on all of this?' I thought. 'Hers or his? How do I separate them, my wife from him?'"

# Chapter Fifty: Real Speak

Michael does say, "He is using wood and cardboard even though I have encouraged him to use canvas. I'm not good enough, he says, but he is. I'll let him get comfortable with his style. Then I will try to get him to let go of the thrift. The cheap surfaces, the acrylic, the pastels. His talent is worth more.

"'You must be Kate's best student,' I said. 'All this neatness. Order imposed on the chaos of creation.' He said that creativity is exactly the opposite of chaos. 'An artist ain't got to be off his mind in order to work. You got to be so deep in your mind before anything can happen.'

"Your Suliman is the naturally gracious man. Amazing when you consider the background. It restores my faith. He is committed to the soul of beauty everywhere. Ordinary people turn away from the ravaged streets and buildings, but Suliman sees the whole and the beautiful.

"He is good enough to have a show. Of course, he wants it because he knows he is inspired. He says, 'That's all I care about. What is going on in me.'

"And, Kate, you have to be part of it. Naturally, you are part of it right now, but you have to be present. At the event. Otherwise it wouldn't be right. Suliman says that, 'I owe it to Kate. Not doing nothing until Kate can be there. Nothing.'"

"But you will make it happen whether I am there or not, right, Michael? Suliman's debut."

"Of course. Are you angry about that?"

"No, Michael. It takes too much energy to be angry."

"I don't blame you for him, you know."

Her husband and her lover have found each other and pushed her off the stage. She has no lines to speak, and if she is lucky, she can be in the audience when Suliman is the star.

# Chapter Fifty-one: The Manager

Kate had been the one who had brought the house to life: appliances moved out of cupboards; the electric mixer assembled and the flat paddle beating away at the flour, egg, and oil mixture; the bananas sliding down the collar at the last minute. The rhythms of the washing machine and the dishwasher were the heartbeats of the house.

Now Kate lives with the sounds of the home that Michael has created. The whirr of the microwave and the ring of the toaster oven when the timer runs down.

It is a good day, a day to leave her room. If she doesn't look in the mirror, she will believe in her red hair, her firm arms, her elegant legs. She doesn't have to use the walker or ask Michael to help her down the stairs.

He isn't at home, but she knows that he is at Suliman's studio. Suliman fascinates him. "His purity, his talent, his forthrightness." Forthright. That was the last thing she would have called Suliman. She would have said that he had a lot of nerve. She would have said that he was greedy.

At the studio Michael will be on the phone, the one she had fought against, calling galleries, calling art directors at universities, calling the neighborhood centers, the local newspapers. His administrator's voice will conjure up a large office, a wide view from the windows, an expensive carpet on the floor. Michael will talk up the life of Suliman, creating an artist with the vocabulary of retail clothing, kitchenware, or office supplies. Vice president of words.

When he comes home, he says, "As soon as you are ready to go out, Kate, you have to see the latest painting. I can bring you the sketches if you want. The actual canvas is too large. I insisted on real canvas. Do you know how much a roll costs? It gives new meaning to the term, 'starving artist.'

"Suliman has to be legitimate. He says that wood and paper and cardboard are real, but art isn't about what's real. Art is the continuum, and its permanence is more important than the cost of material.

"You must have complained about the cost of the supplies. I don't mean to disparage your sense of thrift, Kate, but thrift is not compatible with the business of art."

"How do you know that, Michael? The business about the continuum of art?"

"You said it yourself, Kate. From all the little jobs and the snippets of information. It was meant as a criticism, of course. These are a few of the snippets from one of the jobs that dissolved in my hands.

"But Suliman has talent. The soul of art has been imprinted on him, I can't imagine how or where. He says that he liked to go to art museums, but all those years, locked up…. No, it was born in him. It is a gift of the gods.

"How they choose. That's the miracle."

# Chapter Fifty-two: Something of Everything

Suliman's project is called "Something of Everything." Michael doesn't like the title. He wants another name for the holy buildings, one crowding out the other, but somehow kept distinct even in their overlapping.

"'Churches' would be more apt, even though there are synagogues," he says.

The painting sprawls. He and Suliman have bent their heads over this one, he says. It should be a series of smaller paintings. Not that he is trying to tell the artist what to do, but Suliman is too ambitious.

"He wants everything in that painting. I told him that not every painting can be a mural of the past and the present. The old synagogue, a drug rehabilitation center now, on the ruined street is enough. And six churches in one painting are too many. I am seeing clutter and a loss of impact.

"He took so many photos—you would think he could have stopped at four or five—but he says he was afraid that he couldn't keep everything in his head. There is a church, I think it's in southwest Detroit and it is the twin of a large synagogue half way across the city. The two buildings are identical! I had to look twice to find the cross to see which one was the church.

"Those churches are in the world of nineteenth-century Eastern Europe. The gabled roofs, arches over the doors, the bay windows above them. An ordered rhythm. The narrow apertures once contained stained glass. Of course, all of them will radiate with the clarity of early spring, the promise of it. The clear sky, the unfolding green.

"Suliman is trying to capture the permanent. The stolid churches stand in places where the neighborhoods are gone. Silent, empty like mausoleums.

"The half-timbered synagogue is the only building still standing on Linwood. All the little businesses, the two storey office buildings, the activity centers are gone. Now it's like Kosovo or Beirut, but no one is on the street, picking through the rubble. There is nothing but ruin. And the old synagogue. Ironic, isn't it? What gets left.

"The exterior of one of the churches is scorched to a blackness that suggests a fire incapable of consuming, only disfiguring. It's on Woodward. We've passed it a million times, but Suliman *sees* it.

"That's his vision, solidity and emptiness, the past and the present. Vacancy. The absence of people. You look at Suliman's work, and there is absence and presence."

"You are quite taken with him, Michael."

"Life tumbles out of him. Words, colors, images. Yet seeing him walking down the street, the way he struts, a learned arrogance, you would never know that he is polite and humble and appreciative. To see him you would think he is a watch-out-for-your-wallet kind of guy."

"I missed that part of him, the humble and appreciative," she says.

"That's usually what you miss in people, Kate. You would have so much more to regret if you had seen that in him."

# Chapter Fifty-three: Signs

Kate watches the videotape that Michael has left for her. She won't look at it when he is in the house, and he believes—or pretends to believe—that she has never looked at it. She is careful to put it on the top of the VCR-DVD player after she has rewound it. In the video Suliman's words are soft like the fall of water or the wind turning up the leaves of trees. They are for wooing the audience imagined by the interviewer, the man holding the camcorder, asking the questions, his own words carried off by the wind.

In the video Suliman is walking through the woods, a spring woods just before the fullness of summer. He is talking to the person with the camcorder. It is Michael although the voice of the interviewer is muffled and meant to be anonymous. Midway through the video, Suliman sits down on the trunk of a fallen tree as if this were a daily stopping place where he contemplated the life of the woods with or without a camcorder.

"I never dreamed, not in my whole life, I did not have a hope that I would be anything but a left-behind person. So what is happening now is amazing when I think about it. And I think about it all the time."

The interviewer's voice rises in a question that is not meant to be heard.

"For sure I didn't get none of the advantages. But it don't matter. Looking back is not even worth the effort. It's not worth remembering all the yearning and getting turned around. Keeping your life in front of you is the only thing. The rest is just the way it was."

The interviewer asks a question about Suliman's discovery of his artistic self.

"I wasn't anyone until I started thinking like an artist. Out there on the street I was like a homeless man, not knowing where I wanted to be, not seeing anything. Then it was like I got special glasses, and I was seeing the way of things, and everywhere was some kind of beautiful."

The interviewer asks about the photographs.

"First, I was taking photos of anything because I was like searching for the special meaning of what I was meant to paint. Snap, snap, snap. Man, I was afraid to miss anything, a beautiful house on a burnt-out street, a man walking through the field, carrying a plastic bag and going to the place he called home where the windows must have been blown out. That mural on a wall of a store on Bagley, showing workers in the field like somebody was remembering the world before this one. No way did I know what I was going to do with the photographs, but I couldn't stop taking them."

The interviewer wants to know when the process of photographing became the inspiration for painting.

"I started seeing signs. I don't mean religious stuff, but real signs, on billboards or painted on wood and tacked up on a building, staying there long after the idea of them left when the people moved out. They were jumping out at me on every street. 'What must I do to be saved?' 'Our House of Recovery.' 'Gotta Find Me an Angel.' Next thing I know, I am walking around with paintings in my head, not a bunch of photographs of the sad and broken down city. It needed me to honor it, same as Rome was honored by painters and sculptors. Detroit and all its fallen temples have to be honored, too."

The interviewer asks about the role of nature in Suliman's art.

"I want my paintings to be full of joy. Like the one where this white guy is walking down the sidewalk, which is mostly grass grown over. Maybe he's heading to the store. Grass is taking over everything

"This guy in the painting, he's smiling. He got his dog. That's what I mean about the joy. The sun is warm. He got his sleeves rolled up. Smoking a cigarette. A guy don't have no luck if these are the streets he's walking on. He is walking through wild and unrespectable grass that nobody cares about, so it'll grow until it covers over the city. He ain't young. He ain't ever gonna get the break he's been hoping for. But he got his dog, his cigarette, and his tough guy hat on his head. Tattoo on his arm. And the day is his.

"More and more I see green popping up in my work, the new green of spring. It don't last long. Next thing you know, the green isn't shimmering like it does in early spring. You know, the green mist of new growing. Everywhere. Soon the green turns dark and heavy. Like everything, it gets old; it's getting near to being over. But there is hope in the moment.

"I got my sign for this painting set back and stuck on a brick wall of a building where the window's frosted so's you can't see inside. The letters are big and white on a black sign: 'Rummage, Thurs. Fri. Sat. 10-6.'

"It's rummage all the time, except for the grass."

The interviewer asks about the losses that are the underpinnings of Suliman's paintings.

"You don't got to think about what was. Like it is over. Where we've been just gets us to where we are. But listen to me. I sound like some kind of philosopher."

The interviewer—Michael—says that every artist is a philosopher. He gets his little bit in, every little bit he can. Tailgater, coat tails, tailing behind.

But Suliman is the star.

# Chapter Fifty-four: Chronicle

"It's only *The Michigan Chronicle*," Michael says, "but I can't complain. It's a good article, intelligent."

Michael is disappointed that only one newspaper has sent out a reporter to see Suliman's work.

"All the favors I called in, days on the phone talking to people with influence and power. Well, it's something, a beginning."

Who are the powerful people, the ones with influence taking Michael's call? Who would remember the slight, diffident man who had worked for them for two years or three?

"We'll just keep hoping the news spreads like a fire in the underbrush."

---

An Artist's Brush Honors City's Cherished Streets
By Geneva Harley
*Michigan Chronicle*, May 18, 2006

If you ask Suliman Al-Rashid what Detroit deserves besides its reputation for automobiles, crime, and urban decay, he will say, "A fair break." That's exactly what the artist is doing. He is immortalizing on canvas, hardboard, even on an occasional wall of an abandoned building, the spirit of the city and the beauty that he finds everywhere.

"I see the tragedy in a burned-out street and fields left where there were once houses full of ordinary everyday life, but the people are keeping the spirit alive with their dreams of home."

In Suliman's paintings, the noble old homes on Grand Boulevard, East Jefferson, and Canfield, as well as the renovated houses of Corktown, gleam like old jewels that have been newly polished.

The artist admits that he was "blown away by the deserted buildings and the empty streets." He saw the ruin, but he also saw the remnants of the solid structures of architects and visionaries.

Suliman, as he prefers to be called, walked back in time when he discovered the cobblestone street, Canfield, on the West Side of Detroit. "Everywhere I looked, I saw the 21st century until I got to Canfield. Some time machine took me back a hundred years."

The artist took "five rolls of film like they were going out of style" before he had gotten his fill of the Victorian and Queen Anne houses that make Canfield a hidden treasure in the Wayne State University area.

Then, he said, the hard part began. He had to capture the Canfield past and present in a collage "of a street that hasn't been altered by changing times."

The dominant colors in the Canfield paintings are the rose and rust of the brickwork, the grays and browns of the gabled roofs, and the pristine white trim of the window casings and dormers.

"I was pretty impressed with the brickwork and all the detail of the decorations, but I don't want to lose sight of my goal, the houses standing there proud, showing the strength of the human spirit."

To the artist Suliman, a house is a statement about the solidity of human life. He believes that every man's house is the temple of his achievements. "Some just have better breaks, maybe more perseverance."

"The Cobbled Street" is what Suliman calls the Canfield series.

"I wanted to paint these great old houses right onto the wall, that's how much I wanted to get them out of my head and onto a surface. But there are just so many walls to go around, and none of them are mine."

Although he considers himself a painter of cityscapes, the artist acknowledges the power of nature in expected places, as well as in an unexpected corner. The growth of a new season runs along the arching branches of trees. The cheerful, predictable forsythia, the burst of early tulips, the flowering of a crab apple tree, the pale green that tips the boughs of fir trees make their appearances in the yards and the lawns of these restored houses that have been lovingly tended.

"It's my signature," Suliman said. "No matter when I photograph a house or a building, it's always going to be early spring in the painting. It's always going to be a time of hope."

The viewer rarely sees a pedestrian on the street or one neighbor talking to another in the paintings of Suliman. "It's not about people," he said. "It's about the eternity that is expressed in houses and buildings."

# Chapter Fifty-five: Short Journeys

Kate is driving again. She has no particular destination, sometimes the drugstore or the fruit market. The big markets disorient her; she is afraid of a dizzy spell and of falling in the crowded aisle of detergents and household cleaners. People will step aside and tell the stock boy. There will be a call for the manager, who will lean over. "Ma'am, are you all right?"

Michael doesn't want her to drive. "The dizzy spells," he says. "They can come at any time."

"I'm not going to the studio. You don't have to worry."

# Chapter Fifty-six: Vice President

Suliman is having trouble with the detail and the perspective of his first interior, Michael tells Kate.

"He has a feel for the street but not for the elaborate interiors of the churches: the ornate woodwork, stained glass windows, saints with the light piercing them as their holy visions must have."

Michael is in love with the idea of Suliman the artist.

She has seen this in Michael before. Each time he had come back from an interview, the new job another chance to do it right. Now it is Suliman.

He is vice president again, and Suliman is giving him plenty to do. Michael is busy for most of the day. The library, he says, galleries. He has to see what other contemporary artists are doing to make sure they are on the right track. And Suliman needs a show; people have to see his work. Then he can grow.

"He is trying to avoid his problem with interiors. 'Buildings, they speaking to me all the time, the outsides, not the inside. The outside is forever. The rest is decoration.'" Michael wants interiors. At Saint Bartholomew's, for instance, there are the carvings in the wooden doors and the agonized statue of the saint, his hands clasped in prayer. Magnificent. Suliman wants to paint the solid orange brick of the building and the six arched windows slanting upward, reflecting the soft spring trees.

"No, I tell him. You frame the interior with the brick, you can suggest the mullioned windows, the trees, but you can't give up the view of the inside. The center aisle shining, Christ leaning from his arched Heaven over the altar, the solidity of the pews..."

"He is the painter...."

"The statue of Mary. And the arches, a place of arches and angels."

"Suliman is a painter of exteriors."

"But not lately."

"It's all so complicated, Michael." She isn't talking about Suliman's art, but he takes it back to a discussion of something less dangerous than her meaning.

"But then you are right. He does balk at the interiors. Like a little boy in a place where he is going to break a precious vase or knock over a lamp.

"He should do oils. It must be your influence, Kate. He said they were too expensive. 'Poster paints, man,' he said. 'You know, acrylic. I don't get so nervous.'"

# Chapter Fifty-seven: Sponsor

"The money source," Michael says, "is a *parvenu*, a wannabe. You know the kind. Not altogether to be believed. So far he is paying for the essentials, but he is backing away from a big show.

"I was hoping for a sponsor from the black community, but it didn't work. People don't know Suliman. Too bad. He could charm anyone. Well, you know that, of course. But art and the black community. No and no. You have to go white. The sponsor, he pretends to be French, Bourgereau, but I strongly suspect he is Albanian."

"Everyone is an Albanian to you."

"I'm afraid so. And now I've got my Albanian in his shiny suit. Living in his own stereotype. He always has a check, and it never bounces. You have never seen a more frazzled check, bent and folded as if he were going to change his mind at the last minute and tear it up."

Michael had found his French-Albanian at a gallery opening in Birmingham: "Detroit, Mon Amour."

He has a list of galleries and studios, and he makes the rounds with a portfolio of sketches. He has encouraged Suliman to sketch in charcoal. It's good for shapes and for the subject matter. He will send Suliman out on his own once he has the vocabulary to talk about his art. For the time being, he uses words to sell Suliman. "Isn't that what words are? Bargaining chips?"

Vice president of words.

"He needs clothes. I have to work it out. How I want him presented."

"He should wear chinos," she says, "and a nice shirt with an open neck. He isn't the kind for ties. And don't let him talk you into a silk shirt."

"You don't think jeans would be better?"

"Not serious enough. And a jacket. Linen, a coarse weave and in a pale color. Monochromatic. The clothes shouldn't take away from...."

"His incredible beauty."

His incredible beauty.

# Chapter Fifty-eight: On the Radio

"In the photographs, the old stadium is crowded by houses and buildings, looking small and frail in its whiteness. There are signs: 'Tiger Stadium,' 'Free Breakfast Bar 1-800-Holiday,' and a more faded sign on the face of an empty building, almost erased by the seasons that have been vacant of baseball and football: 'Sports Souvenirs.'

"Our guest this afternoon on *Detroit Today* is the artist, Suliman Al-Rashid. Suliman plans to paint the old stadium in the shadow the new Comerica Park. That's an ambitious project. How do you mean to execute it?"

"That is taking up all my thinking, John. I need a big surface, maybe wood, plastered over."

"How has the demolition of the old stadium affected your work?"

"It's like that dude who painted up all those houses and hung shoes from trees. The bulldozers came and pushed that place right out of the world. But we got it in our mind. It's always there."

"So you are talking about memory as a museum."

"In a way. Something can be there and not be there, like ghosts. Not that I believe in ghosts, but everything that ever was is still around, floating in the background. I am holding on to the memory of the old stadium in my painting."

"But your original project involved the new stadium."

"It was kind of funny. I was looking for the new stadium, but the old one was in my head, and I was getting lost. That's what I mean about ghosts. Then I see what I've been looking for. The new stadium. Don't know how I missed it except that in the city missing something is easy. Your eyes are always busy, your head's always catching up with what is different from the last time. That's when I knew what I wanted to capture, both of them, because I couldn't get them apart in my mind."

"Were you one of the people who wanted to save the old stadium, Suliman?"

"I am saving it, but I am recognizing that a new time is upon us. But we still got the right to memory."

"People who see Comerica Park for the first time are often shocked. What was your response?"

"First time I saw the new stadium, I said to myself that it is just a bunch of bricks. Should have kept up the old place. But brick is the material of choice these days. Then I go around on foot, and I see that it is exactly right. Ugly and beautiful. Right and wrong. Full of danger. Like a sign, saying: 'Watch out for these Tigers. Beware of these bats that are going to send a ball flying up to heaven or flying down to hell.' And, in case you are wondering, I am going to call the painting "Coliseum." From the beginning of time, there always been contests and places to hold them. Sometimes the place outlives the players. That's what I'm thinking."

"Are you a Tigers fan, Suliman?"

"Wouldn't be a Detroiter if I didn't love the Tigers, John."

"Thank you, Suliman Al-Rashid, artist and Tigers fan. I am John Wellman, and this is *Detroit Today*."

# Chapter Fifty-nine: Dialogue

Why are you crying?
Because I am old.
There are compensations.
What are they?
Well, memories. There are memories.
Rinds, that's all that memory is. Even the bitter ones get lost.

# Chapter Sixty: News Channel

"It's PBS. The local channel. Terrible time slot, 6:30. That's news time on the national channels. But at least it's PBS, and it will run again late at night. Suliman thinks he has gone to heaven. 'I cannot believe this. I am on TV.' As if that were the point, his little piece of stardom."

"What is the point?"

"Exposure, not burial in the 6:30, repeated at 12:30 a.m."

"You'll have to tape it for him."

"And then buy him a DVD player. You have no idea...."

"No," she says. "I don't."

# Chapter Sixty-one: Press Releases

Cork Town Houses Catch Artist's Eye
By Jane Blair-Cummings
*Hour Magazine*
Detroit, Michigan
May 18, 2006

He's not Irish, but Suliman Al-Rashid feels right at home in Cork Town among the simple frame houses that have endured shifting populations, industrial growth, and changing economic times for almost one hundred and fifty years.

Suliman first conceived of his Cork Town Tribute as a single collage of the two storey houses, most of them as no-nonsense and as sturdy as the people who built them, the first generation of Irish immigrants to come to Detroit. Some houses have touches of the Queen Anne style with the turned porch posts and the scalloped hoods over the windows.

The artist admires the houses painted in bold colors and trimmed in white or a deep rose. "You can hear the people saying about their dream house, 'I'm going to have me a front porch and a bay window.'"

The result is a series of small paintings where each house, in a grouping of six, is its own subject.

Suliman pays close attention to the neat squares and rectangles of lawn, another source of pride for the owners of this preserved neighborhood that honors the durable houses of a Detroit gone by. "Everything I see in Cork Town tells me about how tough and noble ordinary people are. The ordinary people built these houses and the good folk living there now are keeping their dreams alive."

This artist has given up what he calls the luxury of oil for simple acrylics, poster paint, and, yes, house paint. He has created a fresh palette for the Cork Town Collection. "Detroit has a dark spirit," he says, "so I have been using dark colors that catch the darkness. Still I have been paying my tributes to what always lasts, the trees, the tough little flowers, the sky that manages to be there every day."

The Cork Town project has allowed him to break away from his dark palette and burst into yellow, vivid green, hearty pink and energetic blue.

The collection is on loan to The Next Century Gallery in Birmingham, but it will return to Gallery Detroit, the artist's studio, for the grand opening of his entire collection on June 16, 2006.

History on Canvas
By David Morgan
*Detroit Free Press*
Art Section, Sunday, June 24, 2006

Suliman Al-Rashid has discovered Detroit. When the artist moved to the area, he "took one look at the city and knew I had to paint it." Suliman—he prefers to be called by the single name—is a self-taught artist, but he claims that the once-splendid buildings of Victorian Detroit have given him all the lessons that he needs.

His masterwork is entitled "Something of Everything." He acknowledges that the seven paintings that make up this compendium of churches and synagogues could well be called something else. However, Suliman works by what he calls his artistic vision. "I study my photographs of houses and churches and factories and apartment buildings that have seen better days," he said, "and then I see the sign, maybe a billboard or a poster that tells me what they are all about. That's how I come to name my paintings."

The artist respects his vision. "I'm not taking credit for it. God gave me the eyes to see the signs that are the titles of my paintings. I have to respect that."

"Something of Everything" is a project of great scope. The seven paintings are amassed on the long wall of Gallery Detroit, Suliman's studio/showplace on Evaline Street on Detroit's near-east side. "I'll be needing a bigger studio," he said, "and this place is pretty big. Now this wall, a good twenty-five long, is used up with one project."

The seven buildings in this collection circle around the ballooning purple letters of the title, which is outlined in red. The churches and the synagogues are rendered with an awe and appreciation of their magnificent structures, the balance of their forms, the adherence to the innovative yet traditional principles of twentieth-century American architecture.

From Victorian Gothic to Neo-Mediterranean, from Romanesque to the half-timbering of a late Tudor style, from the clean lines of the Beaux Arts school to the Baroque, Suliman's churches lean toward one another, a labyrinth of arches and turrets, of spires and round towers.

The reproduction of an Eastern European synagogue, with its echoes of a medieval time, is a study in brown and white, the three dormers dominating the building and echoed by double windows on the two lower stories.

"That's when I decided to use a simple medium," Suliman said. "This wasn't about paint. It was about existing and surviving. The human story when all is told."

From his photographs, Suliman paints directly on poster board or reinforced cardboard or the surfaces of beaverboard, layered with under coatings. There are no preliminary sketches. This artist is in a hurry.

"I guess I am the best customer at One Hour Photo," he said, laughing and shaking his head at the expense. "My eye takes it in, and then the camera saves it for me. My last stop every day is the photo shop. I don't even go home until the film is ready."

Then it is a long night's work, the artist says. While the image is fresh in his mind, he chooses from the neatly arranged tubes of acrylics, the jars of poster paint, and the containers of house paint the colors that have been captured on film and in his mind's eye.

"I like the shapes of these sanctuaries," he says. "The world was in balance once, and this is all we got to remind us that it counted for something."

Although he admires the detail of the buildings themselves, his paintings emphasize the scope and symmetry of old churches of the elaborate Gothic style and the Byzantine exotic elements in the Romanesque synagogue, Shaarey Zedek, now the Greater Bethlehem Temple.

"On the other side of town," Suliman said, "I saw a church looking like the twin of Greater Bethlehem. Same round arches on the doors and windows, everything in sets of three. Same slope to the roof, same side buildings. Makes you stop and think that the architects didn't have to know each other to get the picture of where the Lord ought to be staying."

Suliman's favorite church is the low, stucco edifice that is surrounded by the buildings of Gesu Parish on the northwest side of the city. The warm Mediterranean style, the low structure, the broad, cobbled roof are offset by the stolid, wide arched doors and the round windows latticed in stone carving. "A church like this almost paints itself," the artist says. "The lines just flow."

His studio is an austere building. "This is what I called pared-down American, the kind built for working in. The bricks are telling the story, and the windows are for real."

The bare white gallery/studio is a backdrop for the earth browns and the brick reds and the terra cotta of Suliman's palette in this mural wall that is both history and art.

# Chapter Sixty-two: Gallery Opening

"Girls, the celebrations in the life of family are more challenging than Christmas or Easter. We all know what to do for these holidays. We have tradition to fall back on. The ornaments are stored in the basement, along with the artificial tree. I have always loved a living tree for Christmas, but it isn't practical. Sometimes we have to sacrifice the natural for the artificial. The pine needles are so hard to vacuum up, and in nature needles have to fall from a tree. But Christmas and Easter take care of themselves. The baskets and the plastic eggs can be used year after year. But the special events, an anniversary, a promotion, a graduation from school, that's where planning and thrift are your greatest allies. That's when it is important to improvise.

"Take flowers, for example. You don't have to buy them. Some pipe cleaners wrapped in green ribbon, and your everyday rolls of crepe paper, along with a little imagination, and you will have flowers. Staple some of those round doilies into an interesting pattern and you have serviceable placemats for a luncheon after a baptism or a Valentine's Day party for your little girl.

"Tin cans, girls. How many cans have we thrown away in our lifetimes? I wouldn't want to estimate, not at my age." The girls laugh. "However, I always save a few to cover with tissue paper to be used as vases on my buffet table when it is potluck dinner. And don't forget the priceless jam and jelly jars that can be filled with jellybeans or little Tootsie Rolls for a birthday or breadsticks to go along with the spaghetti dinner.

"You can be your own party planner, girls, if you see the endless possibilities of daily objects. You will never be caught unawares." The girls look bewildered at the use of the word "unawares." "Off guard. You will never be caught off guard."

"Natural flowers," Michael says. Sprawling, climbing, a profusion of flowers in buckets and watering cans. Too bad they don't make them weathered and a little battered. Milk bottles would work, too. Aren't they showing up again in supermarkets even though they are plastic? No sense trying to find the old glass milk bottles. They're collectors' items now.

No corkscrews. There will be wine bottles with tops that are screwed off and mismatched juice glasses. Kate would be surprised to know how many people had saved those little glasses with flowers on them, birds, stars. She would have enjoyed the estate sales and the garage sales. Thursdays and Fridays were the best days. By Saturday everything is picked over.

Too late for forsythia without it costing a fortune, and that is too bad because it is Suliman's flower, his signature of the transcendence of nature. A greenhouse or a florist might have forsythia, but there is the cost. Still, it might be worth it. If not, yellow daisies mixed with white.

He has mailed a thousand postcards. Other gallery owners were pretty generous about sharing their mailing lists. "Once you are on the inside of the art scene, Kate, it's nothing but fellowship. And generosity."

Suliman wants "Coming Soon" to represent his art on the announcement of the studio opening: the stark and simple painting of the train bearing down the deserted tracks of Michigan Central, each one angling off into a direction that is never traveled; the relentless, single headlight of the engine.

But Michael says no. He wants something with a wider appeal, the collage, "Something of Everything," the churches and the abandoned synagogues of old Detroit.

Suliman doesn't argue. Michael appreciates that. He appreciates the deference and the acceptance of his expertise.

"It makes everything worth it," he says. "All the false starts. I used to blame myself, but it was the right combination that was lacking. Suliman is the ingredient that was missing."

The gallery opening is on a Friday night, from six until ten o'clock because the days are long, and people won't mind coming to Hamtramck on a July night when all the shops and bakeries and little Polish restaurants are open. The white studio in the evening light will be particularly dramatic. Suliman will be wearing white-white slacks and a linen shirt. Sandals, naturally. Michael has an open shirt for himself as well, a collarless, coarsely woven cotton shirt, but it is blue although he, too, will wear white slacks and clogs.

Bougereau, the sponsor, will wear one of his foreign suits, which he swears are made by a tailor, not that Michael is falling for that. He has had to smooth out too many creases of the tightly folded checks that Bougereau hands him with such reluctance.

"I have been trying to convince Suliman to invite a woman friend, but he says that this is about the artist, not the man. I pointed out that you would be there, but it is important to have people who are close at times like this. 'They already going to be there,' he said."

Michael is spending all day at the studio. Everything has to be right, there will be last minute emergencies, and he is trying to anticipate them all.

"I can even handle a power failure, but lighted candles in a studio full of oils and canvases—a recipe for disaster."

Kate will come at seven. Michael insists that she stay away until everything is in place. Because he knows her, and she will exhaust herself, putting things to right.

"Suliman and I will do the best we can. It won't be you, but we'll do it in your spirit."

# Chapter Sixty-three: Balloon Speak

Kate's monologue floats above her head like the dialogue balloons in comic strips.

Balloon Speak One: Suliman is the true son of Michael. At last here is the heir, worth the money being paid out without the resentment that accompanied the monthly child support for families one, two, and three.

Balloon Speak Two: Love Triangle. Wife takes Lover, Husband reclaims Wife. Wife is removed from scene as if she were invisible, as if she were sinking in quicksand. She sinks so slowly that she can witness how Husband has become enamored of Lover. Lover sees an even better situation with Husband than he had with Wife. Lover gives nothing and receives everything from Husband. Husband inches his way out of his own shadowy life into the brightness that surrounds Lover. Wife wonders why quicksand is not called slow sand.

Balloon Speak Three: Gratitude becomes contempt becomes loathing. *It is like a luncheon loaf. Slice a whole bread horizontally into three parts; spread one part with a creamy cheese such as farmer's cheese, mixed with pimento to add color; another part is egg salad with a light mayonnaise, preferably one made in a blender with egg yolk and oil; the final layer should be a green pesto for the color element. The loaf will be reconstructed and covered with a frosting of cream cheese, which could be mixed with food coloring. After refrigeration, the layered loaf is sliced vertically and presented on luncheon plates with strawberries and blueberries.* It is an all-in-one entree.

Balloon Speak Four: When a snake swallows a frog, the frog continues to jump with his two front legs, pulling that snake along, which continues to swallow him. Who is the snake and who is the frog? Is Suliman the devoured? Or has he devoured Michael? It doesn't matter. It is a union between devourer and devoured.

Balloon Speak Five: Women and girls come to Suliman. One of them, young and new to her feelings, would stir in him kinship and tenderness, a quiet girl with pale skin, the South in her voice. She would have no eyes for Suliman's work, only for him. She would not speak much for fear that she would miss something he might say.

Balloon Speak Six: A woman, in her thirties, no longer feeling anything like girlishness, soaks off the grime of her day at Pizza Hut or Burger King. She tries to scrub off the smell of things fried and garlicky. Her hair is rolled while she lies in the bath. There are children in the other room looking at cartoons, and she tells the oldest to make sandwiches for the younger ones. When it is late, she dresses. The dress has been hanging in the steamy bathroom to take out the wrinkles. Perhaps she was once a student in Life Skills, and she remembers what to do when there is no time or energy to iron the tiredness out of a dress.

She tells her neighbor where she is going: "You know the number," and she waits until her children are sleeping. Of course, she has every intention of coming back before morning, but she already knows that leaving Suliman's bed is too painful and too risky. What if it is the last time? For a woman it is always the last time.

In the white rooms they are dark shadows. "I'm too bright," she says, meaning her mahogany skin. No, he will tell her. "You're my dream-girl color."

Balloon Speak Seven: None of Suliman's women are white. None of them will ever be.

# Chapter Sixty-four: The Special Occasion Dress

"Girls, for a special occasion there should be the perfect outfit, one you had to buy even though you couldn't afford it. Perhaps you put it in layaway, but in these times of credit cards, I can't imagine the intimate act of layaway: the dress wrapped in tissue paper, tagged with your name on a shelf or in a plastic bag hanging in the back room. At least that's the way it was in my day. Each week a sum of money would be set aside, and on a Saturday you would go to the shop or department store and pay the money on the dress you wanted so much. Perhaps you would ask to see it to be sure it was worth waiting for and watch the saleswoman or the manager mark off another five or ten dollars.

"Every time you wore that dress, you would think of all the time you waited, and it would add to the pleasure of wearing it. As people used to say, it is worth its weight in gold.

"Imagine the dress. If the dress were mine, I would only wear it once. Yes, I know that is a little surprising after all the lectures about getting the most for your money, but this dress and this occasion will be so special in your mind that you will never want to separate them. Like the bridal gown, worn only once and packed away so that on a day when you run across it in the basement or the storage closet, you are surprised at its elegance and the memory of its cost."

# Chapter Sixty-five: Arrival

Tonight if she were to go the gallery opening, she would pick a dress from the past when she would strut into a room, sexy all the time. Or she would pick a dress from a time of innocence.

The dress could be the one she let fall to the floor on that first night with Casey.

She might wear the long black sheath with a single shoulder strap. When she had worn it, she had curled and parted her red hair and let it fall loose on her naked shoulders. She wore it for a man who had called her a garden-variety whore: "I can get one like her anywhere"—and she was going to show him something about variety. She had sewed rhinestones on the strap to bring attention to the absence of the other strap. "You are a knockout," he had said. He was old enough to appreciate the vulgar sexiness of Rita Hayworth.

Not the black dress. She wanted to be herself if she went to the gallery opening. That was all she had to rely on.

Michael had been gone all day, and the quiet of the house had made her luxuriously drowsy. Tomorrow would be the day after the gallery showing, and the days and nights would begin the slow deflation that follows a great event.

She would be sorry to miss the excitement. Even if the crowd were small, Michael would puff and expand and fill the room with importance. It was something he could do for two hours. No matter what, it wouldn't be a failure for either one of them, Suliman or Michael.

Suliman would be like the sun, the dark sun rimmed in gold as if the moon had stopped during an eclipse. He would be as spectacular as one of his paintings, and no one could fail to notice him. Ten people or one hundred people, they would be drawn to him. He would receive them, wide and expansive. The irresistible Suliman.

She should bring some evil into the garden created by Michael and Suliman. She had every right. She was the beginning.

Michael wanted the earlier paintings to be shown in a room less accessible to the browsers and art critics and the columnists who were trying to spin Detroit into the Renaissance City. He called the room the Fall from Eden as if the gray solidity of the city had once been a paradise. She would stand before the paintings of the ruins without the promise of redemption. They were small paintings, wet gray, rusted brick, red smoke stacks against the flat blue Midwestern sky; the dark tangle of scrub trees growing in the trash and rubble of what had once been garbage and discards. A church scorched like it had been burning for a thousand years, only the building is still standing, black with smoke. A party store on a street where there is not a single car and no parties going on.

If Kate went to the gallery opening, she would stay in the Fall from Eden room in the sundress she was wearing on the bus when she knew that there was menace in the world, menace which she could never avoid and from which she had never been able to separate herself. She would bring the taint of that day into the room because she was innocent before that bus ride, and she was beautiful in the sundress with the wide skirts and the spaghetti straps.

That would be the dress she would wear at the gallery opening, but the dress would be purple or fuchsia because they were colors a woman would wear, but not a girl. The profound color would work against the tailoring of the dress, but that was the point: purity and impurity.

She would stand in front of the painting, "O'Blivion's, Cork Town Cafe." The sign, green on a brick wall, would inform the man and the woman looking at the painting and drinking wine from juice glasses where it was located in the bleak city.

If Kate were to go to the gallery opening, she would wear the yellow sundress that had turned purple or fuchsia with knowledge, and her feet would be bare. Or she would wear slippers. Slippers would show that she has been ill, and that she has been pushed aside by Michael and Suliman with their heavy clogs of leather and wood. Terry cloth slippers with some of the loops unraveling and the heels flapping.

Suliman would come to where she was waiting in the room dedicated to the time after Eden. He would hand her a glass with a daisy in it. And they would talk.

"*I should have kissed you the first time, a pure and happy kiss because you were the best thing that happened to me in my whole life. I got rescued by an angel with red hair. Thank you, thank you, thank you. Being you, you won't ever believe I was feeling love and gratitude and one big rush of tears. I want you to keep on believing in me even if I can't give you a reason for doing that.*"

"*I wish you had kissed me. We could have been happier,*" she says.

# About the Author

Rhoda Stamell considers herself a lifetime Detroiter. She has spent her entire adult life as an educator in Detroit, which has been the source of her fiction. Stamell began writing seriously when she was fifty years old and divides her time between writing in her home in suburban Detroit and teaching as an adjunct professor of Composition.

## Other Recent Titles from Mayapple Press:

Marion Boyer, *The Clock of the Long Now*, 2009
    Paper, 88 pp, $15.95 plus s&h
    ISBN 978-0932412-775
Tim Mayo, *The Kingdom of Possibilities*, 2009
    Paper, 78 pp, $14.95 plus s&h
    ISBN 978-0932412-768
Allison Joseph, *Voice: Poems*, 2009
    Paper, 36 pp, $12.95 plus s&h
    ISBN 978-0932412-751
Josie Kearns, *The Theory of Everything*, 2009
    Paper, 86 pp, $14.95 plus s&h
    ISBN 978-0932412-744
Eleanor Lerman, *The Blonde on the Train*, 2009
    Paper, 164 pp, $16.95 plus s&h
    ISBN 978-0932412-737
Sophia Rivkin, *The Valise*, 2008
    Paper, 38 pp, $12.95 plus s&h
    ISBN 978-0932412-720
Alice George, *This Must Be the Place*, 2008
    Paper, 48 pp, $12.95 plus s&h
    ISBN 978-0932412-713
Angela Williams, *Live from the Tiki Lounge*, 2008
    Paper, 48 pp, $12.95 plus s&h
    ISBN 978-0932412-706
Claire Keyes, *The Question of Rapture*, 2008
    Paper, 72 pp, $14.95 plus s&h
    ISBN 978-0932412-690
Judith Kerman and Amee Schmidt, eds., *Greenhouse: The First 5 Years of the Rustbelt Roethke Writers' Workshop*, 2008
    Paper, 78 pp, $14.95 plus s&h
    ISBN 978-0932412-683
Cati Porter, *Seven Floors Up*, 2008
    Paper, 66 pp, $14.95 plus s&h
    ISBN 978-0932412-676
Rabbi Manes Kogan, *Fables from the Jewish Tradition*, 2008
    Paper, 104 pp, $19.95 plus s&h
    ISBN 978-0932412-669

For a complete catalog of Mayapple Press publications, please visit our website at *www.mayapplepress.com*. Books can be ordered direct from our website with secure on-line payment using PayPal, or by mail (check or money order). Or order through your local bookseller.

Printed by Libri Plureos GmbH in Hamburg, Germany